DOC

When Dr Kara Noreno's husband dies in an accident, she is left alone, struggling to run the clinic they have established in the foothills of the Andes. Assistance comes in the form of Dr Ross Hallam, who soon proves indispensable to the clinic—and to Kara's lonely heart . . .

Books you will enjoy
in our Doctor Nurse series

NURSE ON THE SCENE by Lindsay Hicks
ISLAND DOCTOR by Clare Lavenham
TABITHA IN MOONLIGHT by Betty Neels
MARINA'S SISTER by Barbara Perkins
EXAMINE MY HEART, DOCTOR by Lisa Cooper
INTENSIVE AFFAIR by Ann Jennings
NURSE IN DOUBT by Denise Robertson
ITALIAN NURSE by Lydia Balmain
PRODIGAL DOCTOR by Lynne Collins
THE HEALING PROCESS by Grace Read
DREAMS ARE FOR TOMORROW by Frances Crowne
LIFE LINES by Meg Wisgate
DOCTOR MATTHEW by Hazel Fisher
NURSE FROM THE GLENS by Elisabeth Scott
SISTER STEPHANIE'S WARD by Helen Upshall
SISTER IN HONG KONG by Margaret Barker
THE PROFESSOR'S DAUGHTER by Leonie Craig
THE CAUTIOUS HEART by Judith Worthy
NURSE HELENA'S ROMANCE by Rhona Trezise
A SURGEON'S LIFE by Elizabeth Harrison
RING FOR A NURSE by Lisa Cooper
DR ARROGANT, MD by Lindsay Hicks
BELOVED ANGEL by Lucinda Oakley

DOCTOR IN THE ANDES

BY

DANA JAMES

MILLS & BOON LIMITED
15–16 BROOK'S MEWS
LONDON W1A 1DR

First published in Great Britain
by Mills & Boon Limited

This edition 1984

ISBN 0 263 74862 6

Set in 10 on 11 pt Linotron Times
03–1184–57,600

Photoset by Rowland Phototypesetting Ltd
Bury St Edmunds, Suffolk
Made and printed in Great Britain by
Richard Clay (The Chaucer Press) Ltd
Bungay, Suffolk

CHAPTER ONE

KARA NORENO patted the mule's shoulder with a gloved hand. 'Not far now, José,' she murmured in Quechua, the only language the mule understood. The animal stumbled, recovered quickly, and continued to skid and slither down the steep, rocky path.

Kara loosened the reins, giving José his head, and snuggled deeper into her heavy woollen poncho. Beneath her wide-brimmed hat she wore a closefitting woollen cap with ear-flaps. With her long hair pushed up inside it, the cap made her head itch. But the combination of fine wool and thick felt was unrivalled protection against the biting winds and sudden rainstorms of the bleak, craggy slopes of the Andean highlands.

Wisps of cloud like grey ghosts touched her face with clammy fingers before drifting down the mountainside to veil the valley, hundreds of feet below.

Kara patted the mule again, the corners of her mouth lifting in a fond, sad smile as she recalled Luis's bemusement at her choice of name for the animal. He had bought it for her after their visit to the famous Indian market at Otavalo, centre of northern Ecuador's wool district. They had also bought each other ponchos, with the traditional red and blue design, and thick mantas, blankets worn by the Indian women in which they wrapped themselves to sleep.

'Now you are accustomed to the altitude you will come with me when I go to the Indian hamlets and villages,' Luis had told her. Kara had been lucky. The saroche, or altitude sickness, that affected all newcomers to the country's capital, Quito, one of the highest cities in the world, had only made her breathless.

Luis had told her of others prostrated by nausea or raging toothache, as the thin air expanded inside cavities, putting agonising pressure on dental nerves.

'Perhaps because you are a woman as well as a doctor,' he had explained, 'you will win the Indian's confidence where I cannot.'

Kara had stroked the mule's soft muzzle. It had a Roman curve which gave the animal a lugubrious expression, reminding her of a well-known actor. 'I think I'll call him José,' she told Luis.

'Why do you need to give it a name?' Luis was puzzled.

'Well, I can't just call him "mule",' Kara protested.

'Why not?' he raised his eyebrows, turning his hands palm-up, 'that is what it is.'

'Well—because—' she began, unable to provide a rational explanation, '—because I'm English, and—'

'That's the way we do things in England,' Luis had mimicked, a gentle smile on his aristocratic face.

José's ears pricked and he picked up speed, sensing he was almost home. Kara arched her aching back and settled herself more comfortably in the saddle. She was so very tired. How much longer could she go on like this? It wasn't only the problems with the Indians, though heaven knew, they were difficult enough to cope with, but this trouble with Luis's family . . . her mind shied away. It was too much to bear. She had lost Luis, and now she faced losing the clinic they had both worked so hard to establish.

Kara shivered and raised her eyes from the narrow, broken path. The light was beginning to fade. Deepening shadow imbued the mountains with a brooding menace, and suddenly she felt small and inadequate and terribly alone.

Then in the distance the setting sun tipped a snow-capped peak with gold. Transfixed by its awesome beauty, Kara remembered that Ecuador had once been part of the vast empire of the Incas. They had revered gold as tears wept by the sun, their god. For the few minutes it took for the sun to set, that distant peak became a colossal monument to a long-dead civilisation.

José stumbled again, jerking Kara out of her reverie. Rounding a rocky promontory she saw in the gathering dusk, far below her, the clinic. She gave a wan smile. Clinic indeed! There was precious little difference between it and the huddle of thatched, stone houses belonging to the Indians on the other side of the fast-flowing stream.

As she drew nearer Kara could hear the pigs grunting and squealing in their pen. The half-dozen goats and sheep bleated and the stream splashed and gurgled over rocks, worn smooth by centuries of rushing water. The tang of woodsmoke was sharp on the cold, damp air, blending with the mouth-watering aroma of roasting meat and baked potatoes.

Passing between the low walls that separated the animal pens from the vegetable plot, they reached some rough stone outbuildings. With thatched roofs and wooden doors, they were smaller versions of the Indian houses.

José ignored the first door but stopped at the second, standing patiently while Kara slid stiffly from the saddle. She opened the door and led him into the crude stable. Luis's mule, which she rode alternately with her own and which she had privately christened 'No-name', whickered softly and nudged her.

Kara patted his flank as she turned from unfastening girth and chin strap. Hanging the bridle on a nail and the saddle on a wooden trestle, she looked in the trough to make sure the water was clean, then went next door to fetch José his feed of crushed maize and horse beans. Kara's worried frown deepened as she saw how low stores of both were getting. She would have to turn the mules out to forage for whatever pasture they could find on the rocky slopes, in the hope of conserving what was left in the sacks until the new crops were ready for harvesting.

Scooping up the saddle-bags that contained her medical equipment, Kara crossed the rough path to the place she called home. As she lifted the latch she could hear Almeida scolding her long-suffering husband. Kara sighed, she could have done without that tonight.

For the past three days she had been out since dawn. Each day she had taken a different path, and each day she had visited all too few of the tiny holdings which clung precariously to the barren slopes. The Indians who lived in those bare stone houses, with their carefully constructed terraces and postage-stamp sized fields, could stand in their doorways and see Peru. As always they had been sullen and suspicious, but they had not threatened her and she had, by offering home-made fudge and biscuits as a reward, been able to examine the children, which was progress indeed.

Kara pushed open the door. 'Almeida, Vicente,' she nodded a greeting as she pulled off her two hats and shrugged out of her poncho, hanging all three on the back of the door. 'Vicente, give the mules an hour, then turn them out will you?'

Though all three spoke Quechua, the Indian language common in the highlands, Kara had quickly realised that those of mixed blood, like the couple who looked after her house and animals, were not proud of their Indian heritage, preferring to use Spanish, the official language of Ecuador.

'Si, Señora,' Vicente grunted and went on rubbing yellow grease into one of the several leather thongs laid out on the wooden table in front of him.

'Ah, Señora,' Almeida straightened up from the oven, an iron box set in the hearth beside which the fire burned. Her plump, swarthy face assumed an expression of tragedy. 'The pump, he no work. That stupid man of mine—' she spoke of her husband as though he were not there, '—he forgot to fill the tank. Now when I pump, no water come. I got no wool to exchange for apples, oranges and sugar down in the valley, so sheep must be clipped soon. But Vicente say, we need new potato seed for planting this year. What we save from last year no good.'

'Oh no,' Kara groaned, 'can't we offer some of this year's crop to one of the merchants in town against new seed?'

Almeida pursed her lips and frowned. 'Is no good idea, Señora. We lose face, and those lazy peons—' her mouth curled contemptuously as she referred to the Indians who worked the land belonging to the clinic for a share of the harvest, '—they see you no have money, they no work at all.'

'All right,' Kara agreed wearily. She had come to trust Almeida's keen business sense.

'Is good. So what you want Vicente do first? Also the yoghurt is too sharp, no taste sweet—'

'We've been expecting that.' Kara sat down on a wooden chair and began to unlace her fleece-lined boots. 'We need a fresh yoghurt culture to start a new batch. Vicente had better take the goats to Rubio in the morning. Buitrón can send one of his cargadores to help Vicente carry the new seed. We'll feed the old stuff to the animals.' Kara sighed. 'At least nothing is wasted. As for the pump,' she tugged one boot off and dropped it on the rush-matted floor, 'the foot valve must be leaking and the water is running back into the stream, so there's air in the pipe.' She dropped the second boot and stood up, pressing her hands against the small of her back.

'Vicente, there's a plug in the small pipe that sticks out near the handle of the pump in the wash-house. Take the plug out and pour in a jug-full of water from the stream. That will prime the pump and get it going again.' She picked up the saddle-bags and, sliding her stockinged feet into sheepskin slippers, moved towards the door into the living room. 'By the way, did you mend the wall round the pool at the bottom of the waterfall? We can't afford to let the animals get in there. They'd contaminate the water and I can't possibly replace any that drown.'

'Si, Señora, is mended.'

Kara paused with her hand on the latch. 'Will supper be long, Almeida?'

'About half an hour, Señora.' Suddenly she clapped both hands to her cheeks. 'Oh, Señora, I nearly forget—'

'Not now, Almeida, just bring me some coffee will you? I've notes to write up and I must get some more letters done. If we don't get a grant or something soon—'

'Si, Señora, but—'

'No more problems now, Almeida,' Kara repeated, weariness making her voice sharper than she intended. 'Tell me after supper, when I feel a bit stronger.'

'Señora, wait, I must—'

But Kara had opened the door and entered the living room before Almeida could finish. She closed it behind her, leaning for a moment against the wood. As she looked up, her breath caught in her throat in an audible gasp, and she froze.

The dark-haired stranger dropped the papers he was studying, which had obviously come from the battered rucksack lying open beside him on the worn leather sofa. He rose to his feet with the fluid ease of a jungle cat.

He was tall, broad-shouldered, with the flat stomach and lean hips of an athlete. Like her he wore a thick sweater over a woollen shirt, and cord trousers, but his were tucked into calf-length leather boots which were scuffed and smeared with mud.

That much Kara took in before reaction to the shock of his presence in her home caused her to blurt, 'What are you doing in my house? You have no right—' Unthinkingly she spoke in English. Not waiting for an answer she whirled round, pulling the door open so abruptly that Almeida, who had followed her, fell into the room, almost knocking Kara over.

'This what I try to tell you, Señora, that you have a guest.'

'A visitor is not necessarily a guest,' Kara replied pointedly in Spanish, her heart still thudding unevenly. 'Please fetch me that coffee now.' Kara put the saddle-bags down by the bookcase.

Almeida frowned, darting a glance at the stranger, who stood unmoving, seemingly oblivious to the under-currents that filled the small room with tension. She clearly expected Kara to amend her request for coffee to include him.

'Now, Almeida,' Kara repeated firmly, and tutting crossly, Almeida shuffled out.

The room was lit by oil-lamps and their gentle radiance, coupled with the flames dancing on the logs, cast shadows across the stranger's face as Kara turned to look at him.

His dark, tousled hair partly concealed a deep fore-head. His cheek-bones were high, his nose slightly hooked and a muscle jumped in the hard square line of a clean-shaven jaw. His mouth was not the thin gash she somehow expected, but the well-defined, surprisingly sensual lips held an unmistakable hint of harshness. She could not see the colour of his eyes. Set deep beneath heavy dark brows, Kara was aware only of the force directing their gaze, a mesmeric power that dried her mouth and made her unaccountably nervous.

No doubt that was his intention. But if they thought to

use him to persuade her to go, they had underestimated her, and it was going to give her a great deal of satisfaction to tell him so.

'I don't know why you have wasted your time and mine by coming here,' she said in Spanish, with a calmness she was far from feeling. 'I made it quite plain to Mr Medina that I intend to stay.'

'Mr Medina?' The stranger spoke for the first time, his voice deep and measured. But she was not deceived by his coolly polite manner, nor by the note of query. Did they really think that sending a good-looking man with a pleasant voice would change her mind? Was he a messenger? Bait? Or had they decided to lean a little harder?

Kara had to admit she felt oddly threatened by his steady gaze and the aura of male strength, a kind of animal magnetism, that emanated from him.

'Is this your idea of a game?' she demanded, anger overcoming her defensiveness. 'You know as well as I do Mr Medina is one of the solicitors dealing with my husband's family's business affairs.' Kara was unconsciously twisting the fine gold band on her wedding finger as she spoke. The stranger's eyes followed the movement, making her aware of what she was doing. She immediately dropped her hands to her side, pulled her sweater down, then pushed one hand into the pocket of her green cords, while with the other she swept several tendrils of corn-coloured hair off her face. Her fingers strayed diffidently to the rough knot at the back of her head from which they had escaped.

'You are alone here?'

The question, uttered in the same deep, distant tone brought Kara's head up sharply, the colour draining from her face. 'Are you trying to frighten me?' Her chin tilted. 'Do you imagine that will drive me away? Do you think that making me an outcast will get rid of me? You cannot know how wrong you are. The Indians have been outcasts in their own country for four hundred years and they have survived. So will I.'

Anger flushed Kara's pale cheeks and her eyes glittered as she glared defiantly at the stranger towering over her. 'My husband is dead.' She spaced each word carefully, deliberately. It did not hurt to say it anymore. She was numb. And tired. Terribly tired. But she would not give up, no matter what they tried.

'He is dead and I intend to carry on the work he began here.' Calm determination replaced the anger in her voice. 'I am a doctor, just as my husband was. The highland Indians desperately need medical help. You can tell whichever of the family sent you, that if they don't comply with Luis's will and release the money so that I can carry on, I will get it from elsewhere. The World Health Organisation, the Public Health Department, the United States Aid Program—' Kara racked her brain for the names of other agencies to whom she had written. 'The United Nations, Catholic Missions—there are lots of places I can get funds. So you'd better understand, and make it clear to them, the clinic will not close.'

The door opened, making Kara jump, and Almeida shuffled in, carrying a tray with two mugs of black coffee on it.

Kara turned, her face burning, glad to look away from the implacable face of the stranger. Apart from the two questions he had not spoken. Why was he so silent? His quietness unnerved her, despite her bravado. Thank heaven for the coffee, it would help calm the fluttering in her stomach. She had to appear strong and in control of the situation.

'No sugar, Almeida?' Kara asked absently, still preoccupied with her thoughts.

Almeida sighed loudly, raising her eyes to the roof timbers. 'Señora, I tell you yesterday, we have no sugar, is all gone,' she muttered in a hoarse whisper, darting a glance over Kara's shoulder at the stranger. 'How can I bring sugar when it is all gone? You take the last for making biscuits and sweets.'

Kara broke in quickly, 'Yes, of course, I remember now.' She hoped the stranger had not heard Almeida's reply. If the family learned she was running out of basic provisions, it would give them an enormous advantage. She took the mugs off the tray. 'Thank you, Almeida, you can go—' but Almeida hadn't finished.

'The supper, she ready soon, Señora. You and the Señor eat in here?'

'*I* will eat in here,' Kara said firmly. Then, glancing up at the stranger, she continued coldly, 'Doubtless you are expected elsewhere, and as you and I have nothing further to say to each other, I will not detain you, Señor—?'

The corners of the stranger's mouth lifted in the suggestion of a smile. 'Hallam, Ross Hallam.' He tilted his head, looking at her as though seeing something he hadn't noticed before, and said quietly, in perfect English, 'Never have I been greeted or dismissed with such cold, efficient rudeness.' The smile vanished and his voice had a biting, ironic edge to it. 'My compliments, Dr Noreno. Is this an example of the famous Ecuadorian hospitality about which I have heard so much?'

Kara was suddenly appalled at her own behaviour. Shock, fear and anxiety had swept good manners aside and she had been unforgiveably rude. Though the man was uninvited and unwelcome they were not in a city where he could step out of the front door and within minutes reach the warmth and comfort of a restaurant or an hotel.

This was a tiny Indian hamlet almost 10,000 feet up in the Andes, twenty miles from the nearest town, reached only by steep, rough paths barely inches wide in places and bordered by sheer cliff face on one side and a drop of several hundred feet on the other. Raging torrents crossed by web-like suspension bridges, landslides and sudden violent rainstorms added to the dangers facing anyone who lived here. To the newcomer such hazards were doubly dangerous.

Shame and embarrassment made Kara curl up inside. Her cheeks flamed. Then she realised he had spoken in English. But before she could speak the stranger went on, 'Were I the person you assume me to be, believe me, I would leave at once. But as I too have a job to do, regrettably I must stay.'

Kara held her breath, not sure she had heard correctly. There was some mistake—he couldn't have said . . .

Almeida looked from one to the other, her eyes like two black buttons in her plump face. Speaking no English she could not understand what had been said. But as she told her husband later, it didn't matter what language they used or what words they spoke, she had felt the other things, the unseen, unheard things that filled the tiny living room. Like an overwound guitar string the room had vibrated. She knew, she had felt it.

Kara's heart gave a sudden extra beat that made her momentarily dizzy. 'If you were—the person I assume you to be?' She stammered. 'You mean—you're not from the solicitors? The family didn't send you?'

He shook his head slowly, his dark, penetrating gaze never leaving her face.

Kara felt slightly sick. What had she done? What had she said? She couldn't remember. 'Then who are you? Why are you here?'

'From the list you reeled off a few moments ago, you seem to have written to a great many people and organisations. Is there any chance you remember sending a letter to the United Nations Health and Development Council?'

Kara stared at him blankly, then her eyes widened and her hand flew to her mouth. 'The United Na—you mean *you*?'

He nodded again. Kara closed her eyes briefly, turning away, her face burning, to see Almeida watching them avidly.

'All right, Almeida, you can go,' Kara murmured, reverting to Spanish, as she took the mugs off the tray.

The housekeeper bridled. 'You sure you want I should go?' Kara nodded distractedly. 'All right I go. The Señor, he eat in here with you, like I say?' Kara nodded again, and with a gusty, long-suffering sigh, Almeida waddled out, the several layers of blouses and skirts she habitually wore adding even more bulk to her short, round figure.

'Shall we sit down?' he suggested, and Kara was stung by the implication that yet again her manners were wanting. Then a tide of anger engulfed her, so powerful it made her tremble. She slammed the coffee mugs down onto the table with such violence that the hot liquid slopped over onto the polished wood.

Heedless of the mess, she turned on Ross Hallam like a tigress. 'How dare you! Why didn't you tell me?' Kara demanded furiously. 'Why did you allow me to go on thinking you had been sent by the family? You had no right!'

'No right?' he interrupted coldly, 'I had no choice! Other than shouting you down, I couldn't have got a word in edgeways. Besides, I was curious.'

Kara stared at him. 'Curious?' she echoed incredulously.

'In my job it pays to look beneath the surface, to expose the reality behind the facade.' His mouth widened in a cold smile. 'Your behaviour revealed a great deal.'

Kara flinched. 'Why you—what exactly do you mean by that?'

'Shall we sit down?' he repeated smoothly. 'You look tired.'

The words were innocent enough, but his tone nettled Kara. 'How I look is not your concern,' she snapped, all too aware that not only must she look tired, but untidy as well. Kara was not vain, but it infuriated her that this man, this devious, cunning man, should have all the advantages, especially as it had meant swallowing her pride and self-esteem to ask for help at all. She would never have done it had there been any other alternative.

'If you've no objection, *I* will.'

'Please do,' Kara said curtly, watching as he folded his length onto the sofa and stretched his long legs out towards the logs.

He glanced up at her, 'I apologise for my boots, but I've walked from Lloa.'

'Why?' she demanded suspiciously.

'Why what?'

'Why did you walk?'

'Because part of my job is to examine the background to requests for funds such as yours, and I get a much clearer and more reliable picture on foot, or by train, where necessary.'

'Where have you come from?'

'Columbia, by autoferro to Quito.' He glanced over his shoulder at the table. Before he could utter a word, Kara snatched up one of the mugs and thrust it at him.

'Coffee?' she enquired sweetly.

'How nice.'

The ironic edge was back in his voice, Kara noted, but at least she had got in first that time. Then it registered.

'I could have told you everything you need to know.'

'Indeed?' His powerful gaze held hers. 'I prefer to see for myself.'

'Don't you trust me?' Kara demanded, her smouldering anger flaring once more.

'Why should I?' came the calm reply. 'I don't know you.'

'Let's get something straight, I'm not asking for money out of *your* pocket,' Kara raged, 'nor am I planning to line my own and disappear—' she broke off, shaking her head, and began to laugh helplessly.

He watched her for a moment. 'Have I said something amusing?'

Kara shook her head, 'Not really. It's just the irony of the situation. In the twelve months since Luis died I have kept the clinic going only by using what little money remained in my private account. Because of the legal battle over Luis's will I haven't had one cent from his estate. Besides being virtually broke, I've had to try and maintain my husband's policy of growing all our own food, not only for economic reasons, but to encourage the Indians to grow a wider variety of crops. I'm also supposed to visit all the families scattered over the slopes and high plains in this area at least once every six weeks, as well as dealing with the day to day running of the clinic for the Indians who do trust me enough to come here.' Kara raised her head, her eyes bright with unshed tears. 'Then you turn up. You don't bother to introduce yourself—'

'I told your housekeeper my name and that of the organisation I represent,' he interrupted in the same calm, cold manner he had used since her arrival, which seemed calculated to unnerve and undermine her. He was like a robot. Had he no compassion? No understanding?

'You did not tell *me*. You allowed me to assume you were someone else entirely, and when at last your real identity was clear, you practically accused me of trying to obtain money under false pretences. Yes, I'm laughing, Mr Hallam, because if I didn't—' Kara broke off, pressing her lips together tightly to stop them trembling. The lump in her throat threatened to choke her. She sipped her coffee, clasping the mug in both hands, hating him and furious with herself for revealing so much.

'I'm not *Mr* Hallam,' he said, 'I'm a doctor, like you.'

Kara glared at him. 'If you were a doctor like me, you would know what is involved in bringing medical care to people who desparately need it, yet instinctively distrust any new face. You would realise that the money I'm asking for will not be squandered on prestigious schemes and modern buildings, or the latest technological miracle in micro-lasers or brain scanners, but on basic essentials like water purification systems, sewage disposal, antiseptics, powdered milk, high potency vitamins, vaccination sera and antibiotics.'

Before he could reply, Almeida pushed the door open with her hip and shuffled in with the tray, laden this time with two woollen table mats, cutlery and two heaped plates of meat, potatoes and beans which she put briskly onto the table with a meaningful look at Kara.

'Where the Señor sleep?' she demanded.

'Sleep? Oh—er,' Kara stood up, nervously smoothing her cords over her slender hips, 'in the ward, I suppose. It's empty at the moment.'

The question had taken her by surprise. Subconsciously she had refused to accept that this cold, imperious man would have to remain under her roof for as long as it took to sort out the question of the grant. She bitterly resented Ross Hallam and his power to save or destroy the clinic.

Then Kara realised with a shock that this was the first time since Luis's death that she had lost control. Her emotions, so tightly contained, so long suppressed by the responsibilities thrust upon her, had burst free.

Shaken by the violent upheaval within her, Kara was paradoxically aware, for the first time in many long, weary months, of being alive.

CHAPTER TWO

WHILE THEY ate, Kara had no opportunity for further reflection as Ross fired question after question at her.

After a few minutes, confused and bewildered, she put up a hand to stop him. 'I don't understand. Don't you want to know about the clinic and the work we've been doing here?'

'When I need that information you can be sure I'll ask for it,' Ross replied brusquely. 'Right now all I want is your appraisal of conditions in this area, and the reasons for them.'

'To compare them with your own observations, of course,' Kara's lips were tight with anger.

'Of course,' he replied calmly.

That was too much for her. 'Why bother to ask me at all? Why don't you just ignore my existence and ask the villagers across the stream, or one of the smallholders up on the mountain, or even Almeida and Vicente?'

'Don't be childish,' Ross retorted. He studied her, frowning in exasperation. 'Surely you understand why I have to double-check everything?'

Kara stopped eating. 'No, quite frankly, I don't. I'm not used to having my word doubted, especially by someone who has only been here a matter of hours.' She paused, trying hard to contain her anger. 'Perhaps you will tell me what gives you the right to treat me as though I were—a—a convicted thief asking for a job in a bank.'

His deep, dark gaze held hers for a long moment, noting the lines of strain around her stormy grey-blue eyes. Then he grinned, and Kara was totally unprepared for the effect it had on her.

'You're not serious,' he laughed in disbelief.

Horribly conscious of the loud thudding of her heart and the scarlet tide mounting her throat to burn her cheeks, Kara quickly picked up her knife and fork and with great concentration cut a slice of meat into fragments. 'Yes, I am, but as you obviously find my question amusing—'

'Forgive me,' Ross cut in, with exaggerated humility, 'it's just that in these times, and in my job, I rarely encounter such naivety.'

Kara's head flew up. 'I 'm not naive,' she exploded.

'No?' He leaned across the table towards her. His eyes, bright with strange lights, bored into hers. 'How do you know I am who I say I am? You've seen no identification. I offered no credentials, and you have not asked for them.'

Kara paled as she realised the shocking truth in his statement.

'As for the rest, hadn't it ever occurred to you that funding organisations such as the one I work for could be considered a source of easy money to anyone with sufficient nerve and cunning?'

Kara was perplexed. 'What do you mean?'

'Oh come on, are you asking me to believe you've never heard of relief appeals being creamed off so that less than half the money actually reaches those it's supposed to help?' He leaned back. 'And what about food and medicines sent out to famine, flood or earthquake victims, that vanish en route, only to turn up on the black market?'

'Of course I have,' Kara said impatiently, still not understanding.

Ross smiled cynically, and suddenly it was clear. 'You surely can't think that I—'

His expression was implacable. 'Why not?'

'But you *can't*—it's a terrible, wicked thing to do.'

'Yet it is done,' he interrupted, 'and frequently. It's a sad fact that money donated by local, national or international bodies rarely reaches the people for whom it is intended intact.'

'And you think that *I*—?' Kara began, torn between rage and tears. How could he? How *dare* he?

'No, I don't,' Ross sounded surprised and vaguely irritated. 'But now you know the reason I have to check everything out. So can we get on?'

'No,' Kara said quietly. To see Ross Hallam startled gave her a moment's fierce joy.

He recovered instantly. 'Oh for heaven's sake, you're not going to sulk, are you?'

'Certainly not.' Kara was quite calm now. 'But before we go any further, I want to see your passport and the letter I wrote.'

Ross eyed her thoughtfully, and Kara had to resist the urge to look away from his penetrating gaze that challenged and taunted her, while his mouth twisted ironically.

Pushing his chair back, he leaned over the sofa and reached into his rucksack to pull out a leather notecase. Sitting down again he opened it.

'Driver's licence, banker's card, vaccination certificates and passport,' he tossed them one at a time across the table at her.

Kara glanced briefly at the documents, picking up only the passport, which she opened. It stated that Ross Ian Hallam was thirty-six, British and single, was a medical practitioner, stood six feet three inches tall, had black hair, brown eyes and no distinguishing marks.

Kara felt his gaze on her and concentrated hard on the much-stamped passport.

'One thing has changed since that was issued,' he said casually.

Kara swallowed. So he was married. That was of no concern or interest to her. If she felt anything at all it was sympathy for his wife. How any woman could put up with—

'I have a scar on my right hip. I was mugged in Bogota.'

'A scar?' Kara repeated involuntarily.

'That's right, my assailant had a knife.' He tilted his head sideways. 'Why? What were you thinking?'

'Nothing, nothing,' Kara said quickly, a little flustered.

'Don't you believe me? Do you want to see it?' He half-rose from the table, lifting the bottom of his sweater.

'No, thank you,' Kara answered firmly, feeling the warmth in her cheeks and hating Ross Hallam for the ease with which he could disconcert her. 'Where is the letter?' she demanded.

'I don't have it,' he replied simply.

'What do you mean, you don't have it?'

'Exactly that. I presume you sent it to New York?'

Kara nodded.

'Well, I have been in South America for the past eight months.'

'Then how—?'

'When I finished the work I was doing in Colombia, I called New York to find out where I was due next. They sent me here.'

'Then may I see the cable?' Kara asked reasonably. The unease stirring within her flared into suspicion when Ross shook his head once more.

'I take it you wouldn't want me to reveal your financial problems to anyone else?'

Kara shook her head. 'Of course not.'

'Then you'll understand that as the cable contains confidential information relating to other medical centres, I can't show it to you.'

His answer was so smooth, so reasonable, that Kara felt slightly ridiculous for asking. Yet he had been the one to bring the matter up, to fling her all too trusting behaviour in her face.

'So,' he pushed his empty plate aside and leaned back, '*now* can we get on?'

Kara stood up quickly. 'If you don't mind, I'd rather we left it for tonight. I—I'm very tired.' She wanted to be alone. She needed time to think, time to come to terms with the overpowering presence of this imperious, cynical man. He had appeared in her life with the shattering impact of a boulder dropping into a glassy pool. The initial shock had been traumatic and instinct warned her that the ripples would go on spreading for a long, long time.

She picked up the oil-lamp from the table. 'I'll show you where you're to sleep.'

Without a word, Ross rose to his feet and followed her through a door into the small room divided up with curtains that served as a ward. The curtains were pulled back to reveal three wooden beds with thin kapok mattresses. Two folded blankets and a thin pillow rested in the centre of each bed. There were oil-lamps attached by crude brackets to the whitewashed walls, beside each bed. A fire was laid in the grate ready for lighting.

Kara set her lamp down on a three-tiered aluminium trolley standing beside a tall cupboard. Pulling a bunch of keys from her pocket she selected one and quickly unlocked the cupboard. She took out sheets, a pillowslip and a towel, handed them to Ross, and relocked the cupboard.

Still he said nothing, merely inclining his head in thanks, a faint smile playing at the corners of his mouth as he followed her every move. The small room seemed even smaller with him in it and Kara, already suffering from strain, found his nearness and constant scrutiny profoundly disturbing.

Thankful that the lamplight was too weak to reveal her heightened colour, she took refuge in a businesslike attitude.

'The treatment room is through there,' she pointed to a door behind him. 'There is also an entrance from outside, but both doors are kept locked unless I'm working in there. It doubles as a casualty unit and operating-theatre when necessary. I'll show you round in the morning. There's a slop-bucket on the bottom shelf of the trolley and an enamel basin on the shelf above. Sanitary arrangements are pretty basic here. We have a privy pit out by the stable. Now, if you'll excuse me,' Kara edged past him back into the sitting room, opening the remaining door which led into the tiny bedroom she had once shared with Luis. She picked up the candle-holder from the bedside locker and went back into the sitting room, only to be confronted by Ross, leaning casually against the doorway opening into the ward, the lamp in his hand.

'Need a light?' He eyed her candle.

'Oh, er—yes.'

Ross lifted the glass from the lamp and Kara was mortified to see her hand tremble as she held the wick to the flame.

She refused to meet his gaze and turned away, murmuring a brief 'thank-you' as she shielded the flickering candle with her free hand and returned to her room. No sooner had she set it down than she realised she would have to go back to fetch the water.

Ross had just replaced the lamp on the table and swung round as Kara re-entered the room, making her jump.

'What—I mean, was there something else you wanted?' she asked quickly.

He shook his dark head. 'Not a thing. But as I'm not ready to sleep yet, with your permission I'll stay in here by the fire and work for a while.' He gestured at the files and papers beside his rucksack on the sofa.

'Oh, yes, of course,' Kara stammered and bent to pick up the two water pitchers.

In one stride Ross was beside her. 'Allow me.' He leaned forward to take the heavy jug from her hand.

'No, thank you,' Kara said hastily. She didn't want him to help her. She didn't want him in her room. She just wanted to get away, to be by herself, to try and sort out the turmoil in her mind. 'I can manage.' She stepped back, and as she jerked the pitcher out of his reach, the near-boiling water slopped over her hand and wrist.

Kara gasped. Before she had time to think, Ross had snatched the jug from her, set it down, pushed up the sleeve of her sweater and plunged her scalded hand into the other pitcher.

The icy water was like velvet on her inflamed skin, soothing, drawing out the heat and numbing the pain. Kara waited tensely for him to make some cynical remark about her independence, her self-sufficiency and her clumsiness. What made it worse was the knowledge that any jibe would be totally justified. Her behaviour had been ridiculous. What was the matter with her?

Reaction filled her eyes with tears and she blinked them furiously away.

'OK?' Ross asked quietly.

'It's all right now,' she said unsteadily, keeping her head lowered. She tried to pull her hand out of the cold water, but Ross still held her arm and his grip didn't slacken.

'Perhaps I'd better take a look.'

'No, really,' Kara insisted, her voice rising, 'the water wasn't boiling, it was just the shock—' She pushed him away with her other hand, 'Please, let go of me!' She wrenched her arm free and staggered backwards against the wall, her eyes wide with hostility and fear.

Immediately Ross straightened up, cool and distant. 'As you wish,' he said curtly, and walked past her to the fire. After throwing another log on the embers, he settled himself on the sofa and within moments was absorbed in his papers.

Kara stared after him, suddenly at a loss. Something was wrong. He looked completely at home, while she felt awkward and disoriented, almost as if she were the intruder.

She picked up the pitchers and, taking them into her room, poured water from each into the enamel basin in the washstand, then replacing them, she hesitated for a moment as she straightened up.

'G-good-night, Dr Hallam,' she strove for polite indifference, wanting to redress the balance that seemed weighted against her, but even to her own ears her voice was strained and unnatural.

'Good-night, Dr Noreno,' Ross replied absently, not looking up from the closely printed sheets he was studying.

Feeling utterly confused, Kara went back into her bedroom and quietly closed the door.

When Almeida woke her the following morning with a cup of coffee and a jug of clean water, glancing at her watch Kara was amazed to see that she had slept for almost nine hours, something unheard of since Luis's death.

Despite her exhaustion the previous night, she had fully expected to lie awake for hours, so many conflicting thoughts clamoured for her attention. Yet almost as soon as her head had touched the pillow, she had fallen into a deep, dreamless sleep.

Kara pushed back the duvet, struggling upright to take the coffee from Almeida, who squeezed past the bed to open the single curtain covering the small window. This was the only curtained window in the house.

While Kara was grateful for Almeida and Vicente's company, and understood Luis's 'open door' policy which encouraged the Indians to come to the clinic at any time, she desperately needed to maintain a little privacy, which was not easy.

Heavy wooden shutters were closed over the outside

of the small windows each night and re-opened in the morning by Vicente. But he often varied the order in which he did his morning chores, and twice Kara had been caught in the middle of dressing. A length of woven fabric from which she had intended some day to make a cushion cover had solved the problem.

'Have you woken Dr Hallam?' Kara sipped her coffee, it was hot and strong.

'Is not necessary, Señora, he up long time already, go outside, look at many things, ask many questions.'

'I see.' He certainly wasn't wasting any time. But maybe that was all for the best. The sooner he saw all there was to see, the sooner he would realise the genuine urgency of her request. Then he would give her the money and leave and she could pick up the torn threads of her life once more.

Kara swung her legs out of bed, pulling down her rumpled nightie and tossing her hair back over her shoulders. She handed the empty cup to Almeida, who waddled to the door.

'You want oatmeal? I made some for the Señor. He a fine, big man,' Almeida said approvingly.

'Oatmeal will do nicely,' Kara shivered, 'and some bread with apple jelly, if there's any left.'

Almeida gave her a sideways glance. 'I go look,' and shuffled out.

Kara pulled off her warm, flanelette nightgown and washed quickly, retaining some of the water to brush her teeth. Soon she was dressed in her green cords, a green checked shirt and a thick Aran sweater. She was hungry.

As she brushed her glossy, shoulder-length hair and twisted it up into its usual knot high on the back of her head, it occurred to her that she couldn't remember the last time she had felt really hungry. For such a long time now food had been merely a fuel, and mealtimes a necessary but irritating waste of time in an already overcrowded day.

She had always eaten sensibly, knowing that her health and therefore the working of the clinic depended upon it, but food had never been a source of enjoyment. In fact, last night's supper had been the first one eaten in almost two years without a book propped open beside her.

Luis had started the custom, apologising that there was simply no other time available for brushing up on the Quechua language, or checking the seed catalogues for new crops to try, or reading the latest drug information or new techniques for treating diseases to which the Indians were particularly prone.

Kara had found it hard to hide her disappointment. They spent so little time together as it was. Of course, Luis had warned her that they were taking on not simply a job, but a way of life. She had understood and been quite prepared to work long and hard to make their dream come true. But it had been far harder than she envisaged.

It wasn't just the physical demands, the lack of facilities previously taken for granted, or even the altitude which, to begin with, made her gasp and pant for breath after the smallest effort. It was something harder to identify and therefore harder to cope with. Though she had welcomed the daunting challenge, she had always expected to feel that they were a team, Luis and herself, pulling together, sharing the load. But it hadn't felt like that.

Somehow, over the months, they had drawn apart, each burdened with their own responsibilities, their own particular problems. Where she on occasion wept or lost her temper at the obstacles that continually blocked their path, Luis remained his usual calm, courteous self. But after each one of her outbursts he had withdrawn a little more, and she had suffered guilt and remorse at having added her difficulties to those he already carried.

After his death, reading at mealtimes kept her thoughts at bay, protected her from loneliness, which in the long, dark nights, threatened to overwhelm her.

Kara poured her used washing water into the bucket, leaving it for Almeida to collect later when she made the bed. Her train of thought had unsettled her. It was Ross Hallam's fault. The shock of his arrival and the antagonism between them had distorted her memories. How could she be critical of Luis; he had been a wonderful doctor, totally dedicated. She took a deep breath to steady the unexpected fluttering in her stomach, and opened her door.

Ross was already seated at the table, a plate of porridge in front of him and a jug of goat's milk in his hand.

Kara's heart lurched as he glanced up. She had almost forgotten the impact his powerful masculinity had made upon her. Experiencing it once more, her emotional defences were immediately raised, and all she would allow herself to feel was anger that he should be sitting where Luis had sat.

She wished fervently that she had brought a book in with her. But the table was bare of everything but the breakfast dishes. Of the files and papers which had surrounded Ross the previous evening there was no sign. Kara's stomach tightened. He obviously intended they should talk.

'Good-morning,' she said politely, determined to be cheerful and pleasant and to get the whole business over with as quickly as possible. She would try to find out today just how long he expected to be here. 'I hope you were comfortable?'

Ross pushed the milk jug towards her as Almeida brought in a plate of oatmeal and set it in front of her.

'Now you eat him all,' Almeida warned Kara, then turned to Ross. 'She no eat good, like little bird, peck, peck, she go.'

'Almeida!' Kara spluttered.

The housekeeper spread her hands. 'Is true. Look, you skin and bone, no flesh.'

'Thank you, Almeida,' Kara cut in quickly, scarlet-faced, not daring to look at Ross.

Muttering under her breath, Almeida shuffled out.

'I was very comfortable, thank you,' Ross said with such solemnity that Kara was immediately convinced he was silently laughing. 'And you, did you sleep well?'

'Yes, thank you,' Kara replied, trying to keep her hand steady as she poured milk onto the porridge.

Ross leaned towards her, his face expressionless. 'You mean you didn't spend the night behind the door, armed with an axe?'

Kara's blush returned in full force. He had recognised the fear she had not allowed herself to acknowledge. But, despite her embarrassment, she was surprised to find herself smiling as she shook her head. 'It was the best night's sleep I've had for ages.'

Ross's eyebrows lifted. 'I'm not sure whether that's a compliment or an insult.'

Kara shrugged lightly, spooning up her oatmeal. 'I stated a fact, you can interpret it however you choose.'

'My, my,' Ross said thoughtfully. 'The restorative powers of sleep! Seeing you this morning I can hardly believe that you and that defensive, hostile woman I met last night, are the same person.'

Kara shifted uncomfortably on her chair, her face still warm. 'Well, that just goes to show that you shouldn't jump to conclusions on a first meeting.'

'You would do well to remember that,' he said softly.

What did he mean by that? Her first impression of him had been of a cold, ruthless, arrogant man. While she was prepared to admit he appeared to have a sense of humour, nothing had altered that basic image.

Kara was relieved to see Almeida bring in a plate of bread and a jar of amber-coloured preserve.

'This the last one,' she announced, putting it down on the table. 'But that no matter, you eat him up.' She broke off at Kara's glare and with her chin high, stumped out into the kitchen.

'Do you eat a lot of bread up here?' Ross asked, examining the slice he had just picked up.

'If you mean the Indians, the answer is no.' Kara spread apple jelly directly on to her bread, glad that the conversation had become generalised. She found the personal note that had somehow crept in very difficult to handle, and Almeida's behaviour was totally beyond her. 'Rice and potatoes are their main source of carbohydrate. But Almeida can make a passable loaf for us from flour, salt, lard, milk and baking powder.'

'You don't use yeast?'

Kara shook her head. 'It only keeps for about two weeks, so we only have proper bread after a trip to one of the big towns. The rest of the time—' She raised the slice and bit into it.

'When was the last time you bought in supplies?' Ross put the question casually, but Kara realised its significance at once.

She lowered her eyes. 'Nearly three months ago.' She bit her lip, hating to have to tell him, but realising he had to know the truth if he was to help. 'I couldn't get all I needed and what I did buy used the last of my money. It was made clear that credit was out of the question.' There was a moment's silence, then Kara pushed her chair back. 'Would you like some coffee?'

Ross shook his head. 'That's a pretty potent brew Almeida makes.'

Kara stood up, smiling wryly. 'It's mild compared to what it used to be. That almost dissolved the spoons! But none of us suffered from water retention. As a diuretic it was remarkably effective. What would you like to see first?'

Ross unfolded his length from the chair and as he

stood up, barely inches from her, Kara was acutely aware of the magnetic vitality that surrounded him like an invisible forcefield.

He was freshly shaved and though his black wavy hair needed cutting, it had been combed. But these conventions seemed only to emphasise the raw, elemental maleness that so unnerved her.

'Let's start outside.' He stood back to let her pass and as she did so, Kara caught the tang of the soap he had used. The kitchen was empty.

'Where do Almeida and Vicente live?' Ross asked, glancing round. The fire burned brightly. The wooden chairs were pushed under the scrubbed table. Pots and pans hung from nails driven into a wooden shelf above the fireplace.

'Right here,' Kara replied, pointing to a curtained alcove at one side of the fireplace. 'They have a bed in there.'

Ross's mouth curled. 'To think I was under the impression you disapproved of the class system, yet here we are in Victorian England. The faithful family servants allowed a corner of their mistress's hearth.'

Kara swung round. 'You don't understand,' she said quickly, 'it would not be possible for them to have a place of their own here. They don't belong to the community.' She led the way out of the kitchen, stopping outside the back door as she remembered. 'Why have you asked me to show you around out here? Almeida said you had already been out this morning, and asked lots of questions.'

'Did she?' Ross asked innocently. 'Well, let's just say I want to hear your version.'

'What do you mean, *my* version?' Kara could feel anger stirring. Nothing had changed. She had been prepared to admit that yesterday's bad start had been all her fault. Now, she wasn't so sure. Was he being deliberately provocative?

'Almeida will have told you the truth,' she said crisply. 'So will Vicente if you saw him before he left with the goats. What can I add?'

'Show me your source of water.' It was an instruction—calm, polite, but undeniable.

'This way.' Kara led him round the side of the kitchen wall and over a rocky hillock to where a waterfall cascaded about fifteen feet from a fissure in the rock down into a pool.

'A pipe runs from the pool to a pump in the wash-house,' Kara said briskly.

'I can see you've walled the pool off to protect it from contamination here, but what about higher up?' Ross rested one boot on a boulder and tilted his head back to see where the water was coming from. He had both hands in his trouser pockets and appeared totally relaxed.

'This water comes straight off Pichincha mountain,' Kara replied. 'The only people directly above us are herders grazing sheep and goats. I suppose it's theoretically possible that an animal carcase could foul the water, but it's very unlikely. The condors would pick it clean within a few days. But in any case, we boil all our drinking water as a precaution.'

Ross nodded. 'We'll look at the crops now. Tell me, what do you think the Indians' biggest problem is?'

Kara was growing more and more perplexed. What was he up to? All this moving about and the quick changes of subject, what was it all for? Intuition warned her she wouldn't get an answer even if she asked. So, in a mood of mounting uncertainty, she replied, 'Shortage of land. Each family owns its own plot which is handed down through generations. Sometimes through marriage, plots are joined or divided and one family's land may be broken up into several plots at different levels.'

'If it's so hard for them to make a living, why don't

they sell the land?' Ross asked, still staring at the panoramic view.

'And do what?' Kara demanded. 'Where could they go? To the cities to join the hundreds of others scavenging through dustbins, living on unfinished building sites, or in hopeless squalor in shanty towns?'

'Surely that's not the only solution?' Ross countered coolly. 'The government is trying to attract them into the Oriente where there are huge plains of fertile land, which once cleared could support any number.'

'It's not that simple,' Kara's voice rose in exasperation. 'These people are used to living at high altitudes. Their bodies have adapted to the thinner atmosphere. Their lungs are much larger and their blood contains more red cells than normal and is laden with extra haemoglobin to absorb more oxygen. As soon as they descend to the valleys they are prone to respiratory problems. Besides, the Amazonian plains and jungle carry their own high risk of tropical disease. The highlanders just can't cope with that kind of adjustment, apart from not wanting to leave their ancestral homes.'

How long was this inquisition going to last, Kara wondered restlessly. Then Ross turned the full power of his dark gaze upon her.

'If their attachment to their land is so great, and if, as outsiders, Almeida and Vicente would not be permitted to build here, how was your husband able to get hold of the land for the clinic?'

'Quite legally, I assure you,' Kara retorted hotly, stung by his implication.

'I was not suggesting—'

'Oh no?' She didn't bother to hide her scepticism.

'Why so defensive?' Ross asked with deceptive mildness.

'What do you expect?' she flung at him, 'if you are going to make snide insinuations—'

'I insinuated nothing,' Ross snapped. 'I asked a perfectly logical question. If the Indians refuse to sell their land, how did you acquire it?'

Kara flushed and looked down at her feet. She had to admit it was a logical thing to ask. But there was something about his method of questioning that infuriated her. They hadn't exactly got off to a good start, but surely that wasn't all *her* fault?

Even so, allowing him to see that his interrogation rankled was not going to improve matters. He would simply write her off as over-emotional and incompetent, and that would definitely harm her chances of getting a grant. She took a deep breath.

'An influenza epidemic killed several of the villagers, including the old couple who owned this plot. Their only son had died some years previously and their daughter had married into another community. Luis approached as many of the village council as were here, to ask if he could buy the land to establish a permanent medical aid centre which would give free treatment to all the Indians in the area. He already had government permission.'

'How did he know about the land in the first place?'

Kara was beginning to feel like a candidate in an important examination. The chill morning air had permeated her thick sweater and warm shirt and she clasped her arms across her chest as she began to shiver.

'Before we were married, Luis worked for the Public Health Department as part of a medical team conducting surveys into the health problems of the highland Indians. The team would gather information on field trips, compile statistics and make recommendations. But nothing seemed to get done. So when the chance arose for him to do something himself, he took it.'

'How fortunate his circumstances made such generosity possible,' Ross murmured.

'Yes, wasn't it?' Kara said tightly. She had had enough. 'Look, I don't wish to appear obstructive but I can't spare any more time.'

Ross turned to look at the clinic. 'Why are there shutters over the windows?'

Again his abrupt change of subject threw Kara momentarily. 'Shut—? Because we couldn't afford to keep replacing the glass.'

A puzzled frown drew Ross's brows together. 'Why should you need to?'

Kara kicked some pebbles to one side of the path. 'The Indians had very mixed feelings about us coming here, especially the men who had been away working for several months. Encouraged by the brujo, the local witch-doctor, who saw us as a threat, they beat up the old men who had agreed to us establishing the clinic. Then they stoned us and smashed the windows.'

Ross's face hardened. 'Were you hurt?'

Kara shuffled her feet, wishing she had not mentioned it. 'Not much, I learned to duck quickly. I'm sorry, but I really must get back.' She turned away.

'You won't mind if I join you.' Ross's long legs easily matched her stride.

'Do I have a choice?'

His deep, rich laughter startled her and she glanced up. His dark eyes gleamed as he studied her upturned face, lingering deliberately, almost insolently, on her mouth.

Her heart contracted, suddenly, painfully, and the blood was hot in her cheeks.

'No,' he said softly, 'none whatsoever, and that is something you'll have to get used to for as long as I'm here.'

This was her chance. Like a prisoner awaiting sentence, she forced the words out, trying unsuccessfully to hide her apprehension.

'Just how long is that likely to be?' This man disturbed her deeply. It was not his size or his physical presence, though both were daunting. It was nothing so simple. He was a threat, of that she was instinctively certain. But a threat to what? How was she to fight something she could not recognise and did not understand?

'Let's just take one day at a time,' he said smoothly and, still smiling, gestured for her to precede him along the path.

With frustration churning like acid inside her, Kara marched past him and went into the kitchen. She was about to lift a huge pan of boiling water from the fire, when Ross's hands on her shoulders made her jump as he moved her gently but firmly aside.

'I'll do that,' he said in a voice that brooked no argument. 'One scalded hand is enough. Where do you want it?'

He was so arrogant, Kara fumed inwardly, still feeling the imprint of his hands on her shoulders. 'Pour it into the pitcher and take it through to the treatment room please, then the pan must be refilled from the pump and put back on the fire.'

If he was determined to follow her about like a shadow, he might as well do something useful. She went into the sitting room to pick up the saddle-bags.

'Yes, ma'am,' his voice, heavy with irony, pursued her.

Kara stiffened, then her mouth twitched in an involuntary smile. Slinging the saddle-bags over one arm, she unlocked the door and entered the treatment room. She looked at the old, scarred, mostly second-hand equipment and felt a warm glow of pride. This was her world. Here she came into her own, doing the job for which she had trained long and hard and which, despite the problems she faced daily, she loved. How long would it take Ross Hallam to reach a decision?

Worry gnawed at her, banishing her moment of lightheartedness. Antibiotics and vaccination sera were vital weapons in her struggle against disease in the community, and stocks of both were dangerously low. Potato planting was due to begin soon, and the wheat and oats would be harvested in July and August. Both events meant the return to the community of men who had been working away, and that nearly always resulted in outbreaks of illness, especially among the children, who were undernourished and had little resistance to organisms brought in from the banana plantations and sugar cane fields of the tropical lowlands.

The sound of Ross's footsteps roused her and she busied herself opening the saddle-bags, taking out the small aneroid sphygmomanometer, her stethoscope and other items she always took on what she wryly termed her 'house calls'.

Ross set the water down by the trolley and, straightening up, examined the small room with a thoroughness that tightened Kara's stretched nerves almost to snapping point as she waited. Let him say one scathing word, make one derisive comment . . .

'Where do you keep your drugs?' he asked.

'Everything but vaccination sera is in the cupboard,' she pointed. 'Those are in another cupboard in the vegetable store, which is dark and dry.'

He stretched out his hand for the keys and, opening the cupboard wide, scanned the sparsely filled shelves. Then he turned to Kara.

'I am supposed to be assessing the viability of this clinic. I can hardly do that if it doesn't have the medicines with which to treat the patients.'

'But that's why I wrote to you in the first place,' Kara burst out. 'How can I treat my patients if I can't afford to buy the drugs?'

Ross closed the cupboard doors and leaned against them, folding his arms. 'I think you had better tell me where your husband got the money to start this clinic in the first place, and why you are now asking the UN and, by the sound of things, every other health agency you can think of, for the money to keep it going.'

CHAPTER THREE

SOUNDS OF footsteps and snatches of conversation, low and unintelligible, reached them from outside.

Kara looked up. 'I'll tell you anything you want to know, but it will have to wait until later. I've spent the past three days out on the mountain visiting isolated hamlets and smallholders, so I'm expecting quite a crowd this morning.'

'You have no objection to my sitting in, I take it?' Ross enquired.

'*I* don't mind in the least,' Kara replied, 'but if any of the patients object you'll have to leave. It has taken me a long time to win their confidence and I won't risk losing it over someone who will only be here for a few days.' She wondered for a moment if she had gone too far. After all, he was here to help. But the point needed to be made. All the drugs in the world would be useless if the patients stopped coming to the clinic.

'Then let's leave it to them, shall we?' Ross answered, and Kara sensed he was both surprised and irritated at her conditional acceptance of his presence.

'What preparations do you make before opening the clinic?' he asked curtly.

'Not many. It's not possible as I never know what I'll be dealing with. Up until three weeks ago I always kept one sealed drum containing sterile towels and dressings in the linen cupboard and after every session I would sterilise a basic set of instruments and leave them in the autoclave ready for an emergency.'

Ross frowned. 'Why stop then? Have you given up emergencies?'

Refusing to be baited, Kara stalked past him into the

ward, returning with a bale of clean towels resting on two folded waterproof sheets and topped by several lint-wrapped packages. 'The autoclave runs on electricity, as do the operating lights, but the generator packed up three weeks ago. And before you ask, it didn't simply run out of petrol, I checked.'

'So how have you managed since then?' Ross watched her with renewed interest as she spread the larger waterproof over the operating-table and, shaking the smaller one open, laid it on the top shelf of a metal trolley and covered it with a white towel.

'I've had to boil the metal instruments in two per cent sodium carbonate. What isn't boiled—scalpel blades, catheters, and sharp scissors—is stored in borax and formaldehyde.'

'What about sterile water for saline or rinsing catheter tubes? You obviously don't have a "still".'

Kara glared at him, then lifted the lid from a metal container and, taking a pair of Cheatle's forceps from a jar labelled *Sterile—removal only*, she extracted forceps, a scalpel and a pair of stitch scissors and laid them on the towel-covered trolley.

'I boil it on the fire.' She could barely hide her impatience. What on earth did he expect her to do? Surely he was aware of the make do and mend type of medicine and surgery resorted to in conditions like this?

Replacing the forceps in the jar, Kara picked up one of the lint-wrapped parcels and, opening it carefully so that her hands touched neither the inner surface of the lint or the instruments it contained, she spread them on the trolley and quickly covered them with a fresh towel.

Taking a last look around Kara unlocked the outside door, greeting in Quechua the people shuffling about on the path. They were mostly women, some with children, but Kara glimpsed one young man and an older one at the back.

As Ross appeared behind her in the doorway all talking ceased abruptly. The Indians stared at the tall stranger, their slanted eyes suspicious, their wide, flat faces hard and closed.

'This is Dr Hallam,' Kara introduced Ross. 'He will be here for a short while to see how the clinic works and how we may be of more help to you.'

Several of the women exchanged glances and the older man at the back spat deliberately and turned away.

'Do you recognise him?' Ross murmured urgently in Kara's ear.

She nodded, her eyes troubled. 'That's the brujo.'

Ross hardly raised his voice but it was clearly audible above the mutters and scuffling feet. 'I see you, wise one.' The man hesitated but did not turn.

Kara glanced up in surprise at Ross, who had moved forward to stand beside her. 'What are you doing?' she whispered.

He ignored her, concentrating on the man whose back was towards him. 'You see what others cannot, the wisdom and secrets of the ancestors are yours, but hear me well.' Ross paused and to Kara's utter amazement slipped one arm round her shoulders. 'I am not blind, and I know you.'

Though she realised his words had a special significance, Kara could not fathom their meaning.

Her whole awareness was captured by the weight and pressure of his arm around her and his warm, strong fingers on her shoulder. For one blissful moment she felt totally safe, protected. The urge to lean against him, to draw some of his strength and vitality into herself, was almost overwhelming.

The brujo turned his head and looked briefly at Ross. Then, with studied contempt walked away towards the village.

Kara almost staggered as Ross dropped his arm and

stepped back, sliding his hands into his pockets, as distant and enigmatic as before.

Denying her body's betrayal, shaken by the need for help and comfort that had welled up within her, Kara turned to go back into the treatment room. 'What was all that about?' she asked lightly as she passed Ross.

'Just a warning,' he replied. But against whom or what she had no chance to discover, for the first patient followed them in.

The woman wore no shoes. Her calloused feet were gnarled and dirty. Her heavy black skirt reached midway down her thick calves and over it she wore a purplish blanket, folded in half and pinned cape-wise at the front. Her blue-black hair straggled over her shoulders from a centre parting. She carried a child of about two on her back in a sling made out of a length of cloth tied around her shoulders in a knot.

She tugged the sling over her head and cradled the fretful child in her arms, pointing with a grubby finger to its red, swollen mouth.

Questioning the woman Kara learned that the child, a little boy, had been feverish and restless for several days, refusing to eat. She spread a clean towel on the waterproof sheet and asked the mother to lay the boy on the operating-table. While she did so Kara poured hot water into a basin and washed her hands.

As she gently coaxed the child to open his mouth, Kara saw, as she expected, the mucous membranes were covered with white spots and patches. She put out her hand, reaching for her pencil flashlight, only to feel it slapped expertly into her palm.

'Thank you,' she glanced up in surprise.

'Later,' Ross said succinctly.

Turning her whole attention to the boy, Kara carefully examined his throat, talking softly in Quechua as she did so, reassuring both mother and baby. She turned the little head to one side, uncovering an ear, and putting down the flashlight, had started to reach when Ross's hand appeared on her right.

'Auriscope.' He had anticipated her, and once again the required instrument was placed in her hand.

Kara did not reply, knowing it was not necessary. After examining both ears she straightened up, asking the woman several more questions, all of which were answered with a brief negative shake of the head.

'What's your diagnosis?' Ross asked from his vantage point on the other side of the table.

'Thrush,' Kara gave a wry grimace as she poured cool water into an enamel bowl and added bicarbonate of soda. 'Though I'm always stressing the need for hygiene, both personal and domestic, I still get a lot of cases.' She pulled some cotton wool off a roll and asked the woman to hold her son's head still. 'They don't seem to connect dirt with disease. They are far more likely to assume illness is a punishment for some wrong-doing, a view encouraged by the brujo.'

'How do you treat it?' Ross asked. As he obviously knew the standard treatment, his question must mean that she was going to have to account for every move she made.

Kara had never envisaged this. It had not occurred to her that she would have to prove her competence as a doctor. But if that were necessary in order to keep the clinic open, then let him ask whatever he wanted. She had nothing to hide and nothing to fear. Hadn't she run the clinic single-handed for the past twelve months?

'I'll swab the mouth very gently with a solution of sodium bicarbonate. I could use thymol or peroxide if I had them.' Kara worked as she explained. 'Then I'll make up an ampicillin suspension to combat the infection and hopefully prevent it spreading to the parotid gland.'

She emptied the bowls into a slop-bucket and dropped

the cotton wool into another. Then she washed and dried her hands once more before opening the drug cupboard and taking out a bottle containing the paed-iatric strength dosage of antibiotic.

'Wouldn't amoxycillin be a better choice?'

'It would indeed. Taken orally it produces much higher blood and tissue concentrations,' Kara agreed coolly. 'Only it's more expensive, less stable, and I happen to have run out.' Unscrewing the cap she added a measured amount of cold, boiled water to the powder in the bottle. Then, replacing the cap, shook the cream-coloured mixture hard.

'What about the possibility of alternative diagnosis?' Ross demanded. 'Acute streptococcal throat, for example, or even diphtheria?'

'I immunised this child against diphtheria over eight-een months ago,' Kara replied, 'but that fact aside, and despite the disease being more prevalent in autumn and winter, and we are well into spring, the spots inside the child's mouth bear no resemblance to the yellow or greyish white membrane typical of diphtheria. There is no cervical adenitis, no abdominal colic, vomiting or exudate on the tonsils, and no recent history of sore throat in the family, which is why I ruled out both alternatives.'

Kara undid the cap once more and, while the mother watched, stony-faced, poured out a spoonful of the mixture. Then she coaxed the boy into opening his mouth and praised him as he swallowed the medicine.

After listening to Kara's instructions concerning dos-age and cleanliness, the woman picked up her child and left, clutching the bottle of antibiotic and the plastic spoon.

As she turned from the door Kara caught Ross regard-ing her with the same thoughtful expression she had glimpsed once before. It was a strange combination of almost clinical detachment with the frankly appraising stare of a predatory male. She looked away at once, her cheeks hot, and moved quickly to the bench. Picking up a ballpoint pen she began to enter details of treatment on a card taken from an oblong box, only to have the pen run dry after her first word.

Why did he look at her like that? And why did it disturb her so? She tried the pen again, pressing harder, but it still refused to write.

Then Ross was behind her, so close she could feel his warm breath on her neck.

'Try this.' His hand came around her right shoulder, proffering a silver-cased biro.

'Thanks,' Kara managed, keeping her eyes on the card, seeing nothing. She did not dare look round. He was too near. He was testing her, probing her defences. She had told him, how angrily she had told him. She was not naive. She knew this was a game, but she had never played it. She had never known this hyper-awareness with Luis, never experienced, she realised with sadness and shock, the half-dread, half-longing this ruthless, arrogant stranger stirred in her. She did not know the rules. Yet even if she did it would serve no purpose, for she somehow knew that if it suited him, Ross Hallam would break every one.

As she took the pen, his fingers brushed hers—whether by accident or design she had no way of knowing. But his touch was electric and she flinched, blushing furiously at her own reaction. 'Dr Hallam,' she began, trying to be matter of fact, 'I am trying to conduct a surgery.'

A scuffle at the door made them both swing round and the moment passed.

The young man on the threshold glared suspiciously at Ross and thrust his arm towards Kara, pulling aside his poncho to reveal a grubby bandage which stretched from wrist to elbow.

'It is time this comes off,' he muttered. 'I must work. I

cannot wait with these women.'

'Would you mind fetching a chair from the ward?' Kara asked Ross, as she pushed the young man's poncho back over his shoulder and rolled up his shirt sleeve. She peeled off the two strips of adhesive plaster holding the bandage secure, unwinding it until she reached a thick pad of gauze. 'Don't move that,' she warned the young man as she lifted the bandage clear, careful not to disturb the dressing.

Ross returned with the chair.

'Sit down,' Kara directed the Indian, 'and rest your arm on the table.'

The young man did as he was told, glancing uneasily between Ross and Kara, who had just dropped the bundle of bandage into a yellow polythene bucket and was washing her hands.

'Surely that should be burned?' Ross frowned.

Kara shook her head. 'I can't afford to waste eight feet of bandage. I cut off the strapping and sterilise the rest by boiling after a preliminary soak in a weak solution of Cetavlon.' She picked up a pair of forceps from the trolley and carefully lifted the gauze pad, revealing a partially-healed, five inch long gash.

Ross whistled softly. 'What did that?'

'An axe.' Kara dropped the dressing into a bowl and the forceps into a kidney dish. Then, after carefully removing the clotted blood from along the line of the wound, she picked up the stitch scissors from the sterile tray and, lifting the first suture with forceps, cut below the knot and gently pulled out the stitch, dropping it on top of the soiled dressing. She had just lifted the second of the nine sutures when Ross intervened.

'Where do you keep the Melolin? I'll prepare the dressing while you finish that, otherwise God alone knows what time you'll get finished today.'

'This isn't all,' she replied without looking up. 'I've four ante-natal examinations to do this afternoon, and two of those have potential complications. As for Melolin—micro-porous plastic dressings are just a fantasy up here. I have to rely on vaseline gauze. There's a sterile dressing pack wrapped in lint on the second shelf of the trolley.'

So thc morning fled, as patient after patient came into the small treatment room. Gradually, Kara realised that Ross's interrogation, questioning her diagnoses, form of treatment and choice of drug, was not implied criticism, but an effort to understand the limitations under which she was working. As her undcrstanding of his method of obtaining the information he needed grew, Kara found her resentment and antagonism fading.

Strangely, the patients made it easier. Though many were plainly suspicious, his fluency in Quechua and his quiet but undeniable authority seemed to reassure them instead of arousing hostility.

What startled Kara even more was his shift from observer to unobtrusive assistant, anticipating her need for diagnostic instruments, preparing dressings and injections, dispensing medicines and completing the cards as she calmed, reassured, examined, tested and gave dose or application instructions. Time after time she made the patient repeat what she had said.

'It's pointless writing dosage on a label,' she explained to Ross between patients, 'none of them can read.'

'Are there no schools in the area?'

'The nearest is over an hour's walk in the next valley. But apart from the distance, the children are needed at home to help with the land and animals, especially where fathers and older brothers have gone away to find work.' Kara's shoulders sagged. 'Besides, what incentive is there for them to go? They are the lowest rung on the social ladder. What do they have to look forward to?' She sighed. 'As for the medicines, all I can do is try and minimise the risks.'

Ross looked up from the card he was completing.

'What kind of risks? Overdose?'

Kara shook her head. 'I was thinking more of failure to complete the full course. In the case of antibiotics that could lead to the emergence of resistant organisms, which would be a real hazard for a clinic like this. I simply can't afford to stock several alternatives.'

Then it was back to work as another squat, blanket-wrapped figure shuffled in to have a varicose ulcer cleaned and dressed.

It was almost two o'clock when, after glancing outside, Kara locked the door.

'What about something to eat?' Ross suggested. 'That was one hell of a morning. Surely it's not like this every day?'

Kara gave a short, dry laugh. 'No, sometimes it's quite busy. Those days morning surgery lasts till suppertime.' She leaned back against the operating-table, rubbing both hands over her face and neck in a gesture that told more clearly than words how heavily the burden of responsibility weighed.

'How many people is this clinic supposed to cover?' Ross demanded.

Pushing herself upright, Kara began to clear up the morning's debris. Emptying the large basin, she poured in fresh water, added chlorhexidine and began to scrub the instruments she had used.

'Luis estimated it was between five and seven thousand. But they are spread over such an area, and the terrain is so difficult, I don't suppose I've seen all of them yet. As I explained yesterday,'—was it really only yesterday that he had arrived? Twenty-four hours ago she had not known of his existence. And now? Now her life was totally disrupted and she was all too aware of him—'I do try to visit the outlying hamlets, but as you can see, it's sometimes very difficult to get away.' She shook the water off the instruments, laying them on a fresh towel, and dried her hands.

'Leave that for now,' he ordered. 'Surely Almeida can help with the clearing up? Why don't you have a trained nurse? Or even two? The work load certainly warrants it.'

'Don't you take anything in? How am I supposed to pay nurses?' Kara flared, then looked away quickly and collected up the used towels.

'I'm aware of your present financial problems,' Ross said evenly, 'But I don't believe you've ever had nursing assistance, have you?'

Kara avoided looking at him, concentrating on wrapping the soiled towels in the waterproof sheet from the operating-table. 'Luis wanted us to manage by ourselves. Anyway, nurses are expensive, even supposing we could have persuaded any to live up here at the back of beyond. And Almeida has more than enough to do already. The washing alone is a full time job, especially since the autoclave has been out of action.'

'OK,' Ross held up a hand. 'So Almeida is rushed off her feet. The fact remains, you are doing too much.'

'Look, I'm perfectly all right,' Kara interrupted defensively. Turning to the 'dirty' trolley she began to stack the enamel and metal bowls which had held antiseptics, lotions, dressings and instruments, and took them to the basin to be washed. 'This morning hasn't been any busier than dozens of others. Besides, all these,' she glanced at the array of forceps, syringes, scissors, suture needles and bowls, 'have to be sterilised before we start again this afternoon. You go and get some lunch,' she said over her shoulder. 'Almeida usually leaves something on the table. Excuse me for not joining you.'

Two strong arms suddenly caught her round the waist, lifting her off her feet.

'What are you doing? Put me down at once,' Kara

struggled wildly, pulling at his arms with her dripping hands.

'You are carrying martyrdom too far,' Ross said firmly in her ear as he transported her effortlessly through the ward and into the living room. 'If you are trying to impress me, you are going the wrong way about it.' He set her none too gently on her feet beside the dining table. 'Now, sit down.'

Kara couldn't believe her ears. 'Trying to impress?' She spun round to face him, almost speechless. 'How dare you? Just who do you think you are? I've got a job to do!'

'Which you won't be fit for if you don't start behaving sensibly,' Ross roared, towering over her. 'Now, sit down.'

Trembling with indignation, but not daring to disobey, Kara dragged out a chair and sat down.

Ross lifted up the cloth which covered several plates on the table. 'There's cold meat, bread, and,' he grimaced, 'goat's cheese. Do you want coffee?'

Kara made to get up again.

'Stay where you are,' Ross warned in a tone that held her on the chair.

'You'll find a pan of water boiling on the fire,' she said stonily. 'The mugs and coffee are in the cupboard opposite.'

'Don't move,' he grated, and strode into the kitchen.

Kara could hear him moving about. Of all the arrogant, insufferable—how dare he? Trying to impress him, indeed! As if she had the time to waste, let alone the inclination. Then, like a plug being pulled, her anger drained away, leaving her empty and exhausted. She leaned her elbows on the table, her head in her hands.

Why had he reminded her? It was only by not dwelling on the enormity of the task she faced that she could keep going. For so long she had tried to think of neither past nor future. Of course, sometimes they intruded and then it took all her willpower to subdue the panic that fluttered, dark and menacing, at the back of her mind. Just getting through each day, doing at least some of what needed to be done, consumed all her energy.

She had to admit that today she was rather tired. The initial feeling of well-being after her good night's sleep had disappeared so quickly. Instead of feeling refreshed and revitalized, she was suddenly terrifyingly aware of the limits of her strength and endurance.

She sat up quickly as Ross came back with two mugs of steaming black coffee, her pride unwilling that he should see her less than fully capable.

He set one mug in front of her and, instead of moving round to the other side of the table, he pulled a chair up beside hers. After uncovering the plates, he sat down.

'Now eat,' he ordered.

Kara glared at him. Her mouth opened but the words were never uttered as he cut across, 'If you don't have what I consider is a decent meal, I'll feed you myself.'

Kara's hands clenched into fists in her lap. Every line of her body was taut with fury and indignation. 'How dare you speak to me like that!' She could barely get the words out. 'You have no right—you're nothing but a bully. Well, it might work on other people, but it won't work on *me*. I will not be ordered about in my own home. Do you hear? I won't have it. You can take your money and get out.' She jumped to her feet, kicking back her chair, shaking violently. 'Nothing is worth this aggravation. I'll get the money somewhere else. You can go to hell, go on—get out!'

To Kara's horror her voice cracked and her breath caught in a strangled sob. His chair scraped as he stood up and, knowing she could not stem the flood of scalding tears, she turned to rush blindly from the room, only to collide with the solid wall of his chest.

Instinctively she lashed out, hammering at him with her fists. 'Let me go, get away from me, I won't take any more,' she screamed, her voice rising hysterically.

Ross neither spoke nor flinched. His arms closed about her, holding her against him, one strong hand cradling her head, pressing it gently against his hard-muscled shoulder, while Kara wept uncontrollably, her body racked with sobs. Salt tears streamed, hot and bitter, soaking into the wool of his sweater. Her struggles ceased and she clung to him instead as her fear and loneliness engulfed her, demolishing like a tidal wave the walls of resistance and denial she had so painstakingly built.

Her feelings of inadequacy—of being less than the job demanded, her self-disgust at her own weakness, her longing for someone to share her doubts and fears with, mingled inextricably with the terrible certainty that somehow she had failed Luis—were torn in harsh, wordless sobs from the very depths of her being.

Gradually the paroxysm of grief passed and consciousness returned to Kara. Instead of just a safe harbour, a rock to cling to while the storm raged, she became aware of the man. Her eyes were hot and gritty, her face wet, and her nose was running. She could hear the steady thud of his heartbeat. She could feel the hard line of his jaw where his chin rested against her hair.

Then she became aware of an enormous tension in him. He had not stirred since the moment his arms had enfolded her. Yet there was a rigidity about him, a closely-reined power, as though he were holding himself tightly under control.

Kara reached for her hanky. The instant she moved Ross released her, stepping back as she blew her nose, then wiped her eyes.

Kara glanced up at him, uncertain, her breathing still punctuated by ragged gasps. She smiled tremulously, bemused, almost light-headed.

'Why don't you say it?' She felt a wonderful sense of relief, as though unknowingly she had been carrying a tremendous weight which had now gone, leaving a strange emptiness in its place.

Ross resumed his seat, hitching one arm over the back of thc chair and hooking his thumb in his trouser pocket. 'I told you so?' He shrugged lightly. 'There's no need, is there?'

He seemed quite relaxed, almost deliberately casual. Yet Kara sensed a difference. Not a withdrawal, she would have recogniscd that instantly. This was a wariness, a sort of surprise, as though something had happened for which he was unprepared.

But what? He had recognised her outburst for what it was, reaction to months of strain, worry and overwork. He had neither condemned her rudeness nor offered trite words of sympathy. He had simply accepted what had happened as an indication of her overwrought state.

'Drink your coffee,' he said quietly.

Kara sat down and picked up the mug, darting him a glance over the rim. Ross looked away at once, helping himself to bread and meat.

For a moment she was sure—it was almost as if he had read her thoughts and deliberately interrupted them. She gave herself a mental shake. Her mind was playing tricks.

'What will you have?' Ross gestured at the plates.

Kara sipped her coffee. 'Oh, I'm not—' the words dried in her throat at his look.

'You do realise that if you carry on like this,' Ross was quiet and matter of fact, he might have been discussing the weather, 'there is only one possible outcome. Total collapse.' The lack of emotion in his tone gave the words shocking impact.

'You're exaggerating,' Kara said quickly, taking a slice of bread and a lump of cheese. 'Things have got a bit out of hand lately, and the money situation . . .' She changed tracks, a note of challenge entering her voice. 'Anyway, if I don't keep the clinic going, who will?'

Ross's gaze was level and totally impersonal. 'You tell me,' he said calmly. 'If you become ill, who will take your place?'

Kara looked down at her plate and realised the truth. There was no one else. She chewed on the bread and cheese. It had taken a stranger to point out the obvious. She had been too immersed in day to day details to see the situation as a whole. She had glimpsed it once or twice, but her reaction had been to plunge in even deeper, driving herself harder to try to do even more, instead of standing back and getting things in perspective.

Kara clasped the mug as if it were a lifebelt, her thoughts tumbling chaotically in all directions. She turned to Ross. He was watching her, but the instant their eyes met he pushed back his chair and stood up. Once more it seemed he was deliberately distancing himself from her.

'I'd better take a look at the generator while you see the ante-natals. As soon as you're finished we'll go through all the supplies. I want a list of what's there and what's needed.'

Kara swallowed the last of her coffee and rose to her feet. Her eyes were still hot but her breathing was back to normal. The scratch meal and the coffee had done her good. Her head felt a bit like a balloon, as though it might float away. But as she had just been through the emotional equivalent of a hurricane, that was hardly surprising.

Had that really been her? She still found it hard to believe. But one thing was undeniable, she had emerged from it a different person. She wasn't yet sure what or how great the changes were, but already she felt a tranquillity which bore no resemblance to the forced calm that had been merely a veneer disguising her anxiety and desolation.

'The generator is in the first shed, next to the stable.' Kara pulled the bunch of keys from her pocket, detached one and gave it to Ross. 'If you leave it, even for a minute, please lock up. The petrol is too much of a temptation for some of our visitors.'

'Right. Do you use the double-handled pan for sterilising?'

Kara nodded.

'I topped it up, and it should be boiling by now.'

'Thank you.' She smiled shyly, still very uncertain of herself, and of him. Nothing could ever be quite the same between them, though that wasn't such a bad thing, considering the sparks that had flown from the moment they met. Her head felt as though it were stuffed with clouds. But for once she was spared the agony of choosing which of several important jobs to do for the remainder of the day. The choice had been made for her. Twenty-four hours ago she would have dismissed that as impossible. But now her only feeling was one of gratitude and relief that someone else, no matter how briefly, was making the decisions.

She wiped her nose again. 'I'll go through in a moment,' she half-shrugged, acutely self-conscious. 'I'd better repair the damage first.'

Ross paused in the doorway and studied her for a second. 'You look all right to me.' The words were tossed casually over his shoulder, then he disappeared into the kitchen and Kara heard the back door slam.

She patted her face dry. The cold water had refreshed her and cooled her burning cheeks. She examined her face critically in the small mirror above the wash-stand. Her eyes were still swollen, but no longer red. The violet smudges beneath them and the prominence of her cheek-bones told their own story. Wisps of hair that had escaped the confining knot feathered across her forehead and curled loosely in front of her ears and on her neck. She smoothed the wayward tendrils back into place, sighing. She looked more like a scruffy student than a woman of twenty-eight, and a doctor at that.

'You look all right to me.' Ross's words echoed and re-echoed in her mind. Kara stared at her reflection as if it were that of a stranger. Then abruptly she turned away, and leaving the privacy of her room walked quickly through the ward to begin her afternoon's work.

Her first patient had just left and she was helping the second up onto the operating-table, which doubled as an examination couch, when Ross stuck his head round the door.

'Have you got any fine sandpaper? The magneto points have corroded up, that's why there's no spark.'

'Oh,' Kara said blankly. She thought hard. 'I don't know about sandpaper—would emery boards do? There are some in my manicure set on the bookcase in the living room.'

Without a word Ross vanished and Kara returned to her patient.

Half an hour later he was back, a frown darkening his face. 'Haven't you got any tools at all in this place? It's a damn good job I've got a screwdriver on my pocket knife. I want a card.'

Kara unhooked her stethoscope from around her neck and laid it on the bench, then pulled a blanket over the young Indian woman lying on the table. 'A card?'

'To gauge the gap between the contacts on the magneto.' He scanned the room. 'That will do, one of the treatment cards.' He strode across to the bench, but Kara reached it first. She handed him a blank card.

'Thanks,' he took it and turned to go.

'Just one thing,' Kara kept her voice even.

'What now?' Ross was impatient.

'Would you please knock next time? These women may not register on your social scale, but as far as I'm concerned they are entitled to privacy and a little more consideration.'

In the moment's silence that followed, Kara waited, half-expecting a crushing retort.

'Sorry,' Ross said tersely, 'that was thoughtless of me. I'm going to clean out the generator's fuel system, so it's unlikely you'll be disturbed for a couple of hours.'

In fact it was nearly three hours later that Kara, administering an iron injection, heard the generator cough and splutter, then roar into life, settling down almost at once to a steady throb. He had done it.

Within moments there was a knock on the ward door and Almeida stuck her head round. 'You hear, Señora? The Señor he fix. He very clever man, you very lucky he here.'

Kara smiled pensively. 'Dr Hallam certainly seems to be a man of many talents.'

'When you want supper?'

'Better leave it a couple of hours, Almeida. We've still a lot to do.' How strange it sounded, to say 'we' again instead of 'I'. Don't think about it. Don't get used to it, she warned herself. Soon you'll be alone again, and you'll only be making it harder.

The last patient had gone and Kara had almost finished clearing up when Ross entered from the ward. 'Nearly through?'

Kara glanced round, her heart giving a peculiar thump at the sight of him. 'I've just got the cards to do, then I've finished.' She smiled at him. 'Thanks for fixing the generator. You don't know what a difference it will make.'

'I think I've a fair idea,' he said quietly, his dark gaze level, and Kara knew instantly he was thinking of her breakdown earlier. Her cheeks grew warm but he gave her no time to feel awkward.

'Where in God's name did you get that stuff I had to wash my hands with in the kitchen?' he demanded, with the abrupt change of subject she was gradually becoming used to.

'It's soap,' Kara replied blandly, 'Almeida and I made it.'

'Made it?' He sounded incredulous.

She nodded, the corners of her mouth lifting apologetically. 'Same old story, I'm afraid. We ran out, I couldn't afford to buy any, so we made some.'

'How? What with?'

'Tallow and caustic soda. One of the sheep fell into a gully and broke both forelegs, so Vicente had to kill it. So for once we had plenty of meat, Almeida spun the fleece into yarn, and I made soap and candles from the tallow.'

Ross folded his arms and shook his head slowly. 'You really are something else.'

Not sure whether his remark signified praise or derision, Kara quickly finished filing the treatment cards, switched on one of the operating lights, then picked up his pen and a note pad. 'Right,' she said briskly, 'shall we get on with the lists?'

Ninety minutes later, Kara dropped her note pad and the pen onto the bench and flexed her fingers, opening and closing her fist as she sought to relieve her writer's cramp.

'I think that's about it,' Ross frowned thoughtfully as he scanned the shelves one last time, then closed and locked the drugs cupboard. 'There are just a couple of things I want to check.'

He came towards her and, resting one hand on the bench, leaned over to study the note pad, riffling through the pages.

At once Kara's pulse rate quickened as her brain was

bombarded with warning signals. He was too close. She could feel his arm against her shoulder. The contact heightened her awareness. She could hear his steady breathing. A fleeting sidelong glance confirmed his face was only inches from hers, his tanned skin taut over high cheek bones and the dark shadow of a beard beginning to show on his lean jaw.

'I think we'll add Gentamycin, and that should cover it,' Ross decided and straightened up. He yawned and stretched, glancing at his watch. 'Good Lord, is that the time?'

As he spoke, Almeida bustled in. 'You come now, the supper, he no wait any longer.' She stood by the open door, her hands on her massive hips, her round face flushed from the heat of the fire.

'The generator—' Kara began.

Ross gave her a gentle push towards the ward door. 'Lock up here, I'll see to the generator, I've still got the key.' He strode ahead of the two women and vanished through the kitchen door.

'He very fine man,' Almeida murmured approvingly as she followed Kara into the living room. Kara said nothing. 'He good man for you,' Almeida whispered. 'You alone long time now. No good for woman to be alone.'

'Hush, Almeida,' Kara reproved sternly, trying to silence her own treacherous thoughts. Had she not longed for an end to her loneliness? 'Dr Hallam has a job to do, and as soon as he has done it he will be leaving. I doubt he'll be here more than a few days. In any case, he's the last man in the world I . . .'

She broke off hurriedly as Ross came back in. Almeida waddled out to the kitchen, returning moments later with two platefuls of mutton stew and beans which she put on the table.

'Señor, you see she eat well,' Almeida stabbed a pudgy finger at Kara. 'No more pick—pick, "I no hungry, Almeida". She no listen to me . . .'

'Almeida!' Kara spluttered, scarlet with embarrassment. 'That will do.'

Assuming a wounded expression, Almeida tilted her chin to an almost impossible angle and sailed out.

'I don't know what's come over her,' Kara tried to laugh, knowing she must be glowing like a beacon. 'I've never known her behave like this!'

'Don't let it bother you,' Ross held her chair and Kara was forced to sit down. This time he did not sit beside her but moved to the place he had occupied the previous evening at the head of the table, where Luis had always sat. 'It certainly doesn't worry me.'

Not at all sure how to interpret that, Kara picked up her fork and began to eat.

The meal continued in silence for several minutes. Sensing Ross's eyes upon her, Kara grew more and more uncomfortable.

'To get back to where we were interrupted this morning,' he said suddenly, 'where did your husband get the funds for this project?'

Kara looked up quickly. 'My husband came from a wealthy family. The money was entirely his own, the proceeds of a trust fund set up by his grandparents.'

'Very commendable.'

Ross's tone stung Kara. 'I thought so,' she agreed frostily. 'He was one of those rare people who actually got up and did the thing he believed in, instead of simply talking about it.'

'How fortunate his circumstances made such generosity possible,' Ross drawled, but before Kara could utter the retort that sprang to her lips, he went on. 'So what went wrong? Why are you now in such desperate straits?'

Kara looked down at her plate, biting her lip. 'My husband's family did not approve of what he was doing,' she began haltingly. She had never spoken of this before, and the emotional turmoil she had suffered since Ross Hallam's arrival was going to make a difficult task doubly hard.

'You see, the family own several manufacturing companies and money left to individual members, legacies, trusts, all that sort of thing, has always been reinvested in the parent companies. In setting up the clinic Luis was taking money out of family holdings. They were very angry, but as it was his, they could do nothing to stop him.'

'That doesn't explain what went wrong.' The firelight danced across the planes of Ross's face, highlighting his deep forehead, his high cheek-bones, shadowing his eyes, so that Kara could not read the expression in them.

'When Luis and I married, he made a will leaving the clinic and what was left of the trust fund to me, providing I used it for that purpose.'

'To continue running the clinic as you had been doing together?'

She nodded. 'After he died, the family immediately got their lawyers working on the will, trying to find ways of proving it invalid. The most obvious one was to try and get me to leave.'

'The clinic?'

'Preferably the country.'

Ross nodded slowly, his features as hard as cast bronze. 'If you leave, then the money cannot be used for the purpose for which it was left to you, so it reverts to the trust fund—'

'—and the conditions of the trust contain a clause which states that in the event of Luis's death, and any subsequent will being proved null and void, the money is to be divided among the other grandchildren,' Kara finished. 'And while all this legal tangle is being unravelled, I can't draw a cent.'

'What do they want the money for?' Ross's heavy

brows formed a black bar as he frowned.

'Investment in their companies. The world recession has hit developing countries like Ecuador very hard.' Kara hesitated. 'I'm not absolutely sure but I think one or two of their businesses are in financial trouble.'

Ross pushed his empty plate away and leaned back in his chair, obviously deep in thought. Then he looked up. 'Tomorrow we are going to Quito. We'll buy as many of the supplies as the mules can carry and order the rest.'

'To Quito?' Kara was shaken, this was totally unexpected. 'Us—both?'

He nodded silently.

'But we can't get there and back in a day. That means we'll have to stay overnight.'

'What incredible powers of deduction you have,' Ross murmured drily.

'But—but I can't leave the clinic again so soon,' Kara clutched wildly at reasons for not going. It was difficult enough to cope with her complex reactions to him here on her own ground. Besides, she didn't know the capital, she had visited it only three times during her three years in Ecuador. And if they had to stay—'No, I can't possibly go, there's too much to do here.'

'You can't do anything here without the necessary supplies,' Ross pointed out reasonably.

'Then you go,' Kara seized on the idea as it occurred to her. 'You can take both mules, you'll be much quicker alone.'

Even before she had finished, Ross was shaking his head, slowly, definitely.

'You are coming with me, because as well as arranging the supplies, we are also going to see your husband's lawyers.'

What did he mean? Had he decided about the grant

already? Was he going to help? What if the decision didn't rest with him? Kara had to know, not simply for her own sake but for all those who depended upon the pitifully small amount of help she was able to give.

She braced herself. 'Is anyone else involved in the assessment? I mean, do you have to refer—'

Ross's gaze seemed to penetrate her very soul. 'The decision is entirely mine,' he said softly, 'and I haven't made it yet. This situation is rather more complex than I imagined.' He stood up, dark and forbidding. 'In view of our early start tomorrow there is some paperwork I must get finished, so if you'll excuse me.'

'Of course,' Kara murmured. She would be glad to be by herself. She badly needed time to think. Too much was happening too quickly. She got up, bumping into Ross, who had come round behind her. 'Sorry.' She jumped and would have moved aside, but his hand closed about her neck, imprisoning her.

Gently but inexorably he turned her round. Hardly daring to breathe, Kara stared up at him.

'I think you should get used to the fact that I'm going to be around for a while.' His deep voice trickled like dark honey down her spine.

Was this another game? Kara stood perfectly still. Scraping up every ounce of will power, she kept her voice light and even.

'Everyone has to make sacrifices.'

Ross's eyes narrowed and he studied her thoughtfully, his face revealing nothing. Then to Kara's profound shock he lowered his black head and brushed her mouth with his own, murmuring reflectively, 'I wonder what sacrifices you are prepared to make to keep this clinic open?'

Then he released her. Giving her a gentle push, he strode out to the kitchen and Kara could hear him laughing with Almeida and Vicente as she stood transfixed, the tips of her fingers tracing the path of his kiss.

CHAPTER FOUR

LIKE WHITE candy floss, low cloud drifted past as Ross and Kara, astride the mules, made their way along the narrow, winding path. The air was crisp, filling Kara with a strange, heady mixture of excitement and unease. This was not a simple journey to the capital, this was a venture into the unknown. Even the path, this first part of it so often travelled on her house calls, seemed somehow different.

Ross rode ahead of her on No-name, sitting tall and easy in the saddle, a heavy oilskin over his sweater. He wore no hat and his rumpled black hair gleamed as the early morning sunlight gilded the sharp ridges and high rolling hills, vividly contrasting their clear lines and colours with the secret, shadowy folds of the valleys.

As they passed a small hamlet, watched with stone-faced impassivity by the Indians, Kara's thoughts went back to their start that morning. Most of it, from being woken by a yawning Almeida just before dawn to mounting José, was just a blur. She had washed, dressed and eaten breakfast all in a sort of dream. Packing her rucksack for the overnight stay in Quito had been a different matter.

Obviously they would have to stay in an hotel, which meant that she would have to change for dinner. While in practice many South American women held good jobs and even ran their own companies, in public they were still expected to conform to traditional laws of behaviour demanded by their menfolk. No decent woman wore trousers, appeared in the streets alone or went anywhere without her husband's or father's permission.

Foreign women, especially those who did not adopt

these rules, were regarded as a challenge to the Latin-American male's macho image. Pestered and propositioned, they were at the same time treated with extravagant compliments and utter contempt.

But as the journey was being made on mule-back, and as on return the mules would be fully laden, Ross had warned Kara to pack only essentials.

By the time she had fitted in her nightgown, toilet bag, a clean towel and her one decent pair of court shoes, there wasn't much room left.

Kara had opened the carved chest in which, neatly folded between layers of tissue paper, she kept her dresses and skirts. She couldn't remember the last time she had worn any of them. Due to her weight loss few would fit well. In a burst of impatience she snatched up a rich brown, ankle-length skirt of fine wool and a simple shirt-blouse of green and white sprigged cotton and shut the lid with a bang.

What did it matter what she wore? It wasn't as if she was out to impress Ross Hallam, she was simply observing convention, taking clothes which acknowledged the fact that she was a woman instead of denying it.

Within Kara a battle was raging. Her mind, the voice of sense and logic, constantly reminded her that Ross Hallam was still a virtual stranger, an unknown quantity. Though they had developed a remarkable empathy in their brief working relationship, she knew far less about him than he did about her. And despite the fact that his stay now seemed likely to stretch into weeks rather than days, he was still only a visitor.

His was a life of constant movement and change. The fact that though he was a qualified doctor he worked for the United Nations in a job that took him all over the world, surely meant that he had never felt the desire to put down roots. He was merely in transit. Here today to do a job, tomorrow moved on to who knew where?

All this Kara knew, it was simply logical deduction.

But her heart, her treacherous, unpredictable heart, refused to listen. For the moment he was here. Forbidding, gentle, arrogant and intuitive, he was unlike any man she had ever met, and she was torn between wanting him to notice her as a woman and being terrified that he would.

A sudden rap on her bedroom door had made her jump. 'Yes?' she called, carefully rolling the skirt and blouse in tissue to minimise creasing.

Ross's head appeared round the door. 'Ready? We should get moving. The sun's up and we've a very long day ahead of us.'

Kara placed the rolled bundle in the rucksack, buckled the flap and with trepidation quivering deep inside her, followed him.

As they left the clinic, Almeida, who was milking the goats, called after them, reminding Kara to bring back fresh yoghurt.

Vicente was bent over one of the sheep, holding it on its haunches with its head between his knees, while he clipped its fleece with hand shears. Two young boys from the village turned from their task of watching the pigs, which had been freed from their pen to root around the outcrops of rock and scrub, to follow Ross and Kara's departure. The older villagers barely looked up from their steep plots and terraced fields.

As they rode by, Ross watched for a few moments the doll-like figures scattered across the mountainside, breaking up clods of earth with crude picks. Then he turned to Kara.

'What crops have you planted this year?'

'There are two small pieces of land belonging to the clinic on the lower side of the village. Last month Vicente sowed oats on one, and we're going to try sweet corn on the other, but that won't be planted for a couple of weeks.'

'What about the plots in front of the clinic?'

'The smaller one has winter cabbage, broccoli, sprouts and curly kale. Kidney and haricot beans will also go in in a week or two. And of course, potatoes will go into the big plot at the end of May or beginning of June.'

Ross frowned. 'If the land is as depleted as you say, what sort of results are you expecting?'

'Better than last year I hope,' was Kara's fervent reply. 'We lost a lot of the crops for one reason or another, ignorance being the overriding factor,' she added wryly. 'But what couldn't be eaten was rotted down and I've made Vicente pile on the fertilizer this year, so I'm hoping—'

'What fertilizer?'

'Whatever animal dung the Indians don't take to dry and burn on their fires. We also make our own compost. That's what the privy pits are for.' Kara coloured slightly. 'I know it sounds a bit revolting.'

'How does it work?' Ross interrupted, sounding interested.

'Straw, vegetable waste and leaves are added, and when the pit is almost full it's covered with a thick layer of earth and left to rot down while the loo shack is moved over another pit. When that is almost full the first one is uncovered and the compost is ready for use.'

'So you don't buy artificial fertilizers?'

Kara shook her head. 'Too expensive and not easily obtainable. Anyway, we wanted to be self-sufficient. Besides, if we didn't recycle the waste we'd still have to dispose of it somehow.' She sighed in exasperation. 'That's another thing I can't understand. The government knows soil erosion and infertility are among the main problems here in the highlands, yet nothing at all is done to train the Indians to recognise the cycle and halt it.'

An hour later they passed another village.

'What's that pole for, the one sticking out of the roof

of that house?' Ross turned in the saddle to ask her, pointing as he spoke. 'Are those flowers tied on it?'

'It's to show that chicha, the Indian corn beer, is available there,' Kara explained.

'How's that made?'

'The women chew the corn and spit it into a pot. An enzyme in their saliva starts the fermentation process, then they add water and brown sugar.'

'What does it taste like?' Ross called over his shoulder with a grin.

'I've managed to avoid finding out,' Kara shouted back, 'but I'm told it's soupy and bitter. You see that white cloth on the other pole? That's for aguardiente, a sugar-cane firewater introduced by the Spaniards.' Kara's smile faded and her face grew serious. 'Alcoholism is another growing problem, and that stuff can kill, as it's often poisonous.'

They rounded a bend and the path forked. The path Kara usually took led upwards and disappeared around a rocky crag.

The other curved down, turning back on itself, then proceeded down the steep, rough hillside as the mules stumbled and slithered, sending tiny landslides of rock and dust rolling ahead of them.

A few huge drops of rain kicked up puffs of dust on the path.

'Quick,' Kara shouted a warning to Ross, 'dismount and get under those rocks ahead.' She had already slid off José's back and was running down the path, hanging onto her hat with one hand and dragging the mule with the other. When she drew level with Ross he glanced down.

'Aren't you over-reacting a little?' One dark eyebrow lifted sardonically.

'Please yourself,' Kara shrugged innocently as she hurried past, José trotting stiff-legged behind her, saddle-bags and stirrups bouncing and swaying. She reached the overhang and skidded to a halt, manoeuvring José under it, smoothing his muzzle and talking gently to him.

Heralded by a sudden, violent gust of wind, the skies opened and cold grey needles of rain lanced down with a ferocity that was almost frightening.

Though not far behind, by the time Ross had leapt from his mule and both had joined Kara and José under the cliff, his oilskin was slick and shiny with water and his black hair was plastered to his scalp. Rain poured down his face and dripped off his chin.

Forseeing what would happen, Kara had put her fingers to her mouth in an effort to hide her smile. Ross, blinking the rain out of his eyes, ducked his head and squeezed in beside her, a fierce frown drawing his brows into a heavy black line.

Kara took off her hat and shook the water from it, though it was barely spotted. She glanced up at Ross and could not restrain her laughter. Ross turned a slow gaze on her.

'I'm s-s-sorry,' she spluttered, her eyes dancing, 'but I did warn you!' She could only shake her head. 'If you could have seen your face,' she gurgled.

Ross's eyes narrowed, glinting. 'It amuses you to see people caught out?'

Kara nodded blithely, biting her lips as she tried to stop giggling.

Then, as she lifted her arms to put her hat on again, Ross caught her to him and his mouth, at first cold from the rain, and then unbelievably warm, came down on hers.

Kara gasped and stiffened with shock. But there was no escape. His arms were two steel bands holding her hard against his powerful body and his lips, expert and compelling, demanded response.

All thought was suspended, there was only perception. Her heart pounded as, beneath the moving, relentless pressure of his mouth, her own parted to admit his gently probing tongue. Her hat slipped from her fingers as her arms crept of their own volition around his neck.

That roaring in her ears, was it the wind and rain, or the blood singing in her veins? Kara neither knew nor cared. There was no past, no future, only this moment, this kaleidoscope of sensation. The moment stretched, then detached itself from time and spiralled away into infinity as Ross tore his lips from hers.

Kara hung limply in his arms, and Ross's breath rasped harsh and ragged as they stared at one another. For an instant Kara was sure his dark eyes mirrored her own bewilderment, then somewhere in their depths a door slammed and that moment's vulnerability vanished so completely, she was not sure it had ever existed.

'Not laughing?' Ross enquired softly, a grin teasing the corners of his mouth as he released her and gathered up No-name's reins.

Kara bent to pick up her hat, dusting it off with far more care and attention than necessary. 'Hardly a fair comparison,' she said lightly, her cheeks warm. 'At least you got a warning.'

She replaced a hairpin in the coil on top of her head, then crammed the hat on over it. Taking José's bridle, she led him out onto the path. The rain had stopped and the clouds parted to reveal the sun. At once the greyness of the early morning vanished. Golden sunlight in a sapphire sky drew countless subtle shades of green from the mountainside. The earth and stones sweeping down the path in a muddy stream came to rest as the water soaked away almost while they watched.

'Ah, but I make my own rules,' Ross growled softly from behind her and a shiver tingled down Kara's spine as he confirmed her suspicions.

She made no reply and they mounted up and continued their journey, Kara so absorbed in her thoughts she barely noticed the mellowing scenery.

An hour later a procession of Indians crossed the path ahead of them and moved away up the hillside. Led by two men banging drums, surrounded by a scatter of children, all of whom were dressed in brightly coloured blankets and ponchos, four men carried a gaudily painted statue.

'What's all that about?' Ross asked as he watched them disappear round a fold in the hillside.

'They are going to plant potatoes,' Kara replied. 'The saint, either Peter or Paul, has replaced the old fertility rites since the Spanish conquistadors converted the Indians to Catholicism.'

'Didn't they used to offer human sacrifices? I remember reading something about it.'

Kara nodded. 'That was in southern Ecuador. Each year a hundred children were killed so that their blood would strengthen the seed potatoes.' She shuddered. 'Thank God that has stopped.'

Ross merely stared at her from beneath lowered brows, giving her no clue to what he was thinking.

The next two hours took them over rushing streams and through sprawling woods of tall, leafy trees. They ate a snack lunch of unleavened bread, meat and dried fruit as they rode. The morning's thick blanket of cloud had broken up into fluffy cotton wool balls that floated along on a gentle breeze. The sun grew warm and as Kara lifted her face to its golden light, thinking of apple blossom and primroses, Ross called, 'Almost like an English spring, isn't it?' and she marvelled again how his thoughts so often seemed to parallel her own.

Don't get carried away, the small voice of logic warned. So once in a while your thoughts coincide. That's all it is, coincidence. It doesn't mean a thing. Most of the time Ross Hallam is as readable as a blank wall, and about as yielding.

They entered the capital from the south west, leaving

the mules to be fed and watered at stables run by a mestizo family on the edge of the city.

Then, carrying the rucksacks and saddle-bags, they walked through the narrow cobbled streets off which led graceful arcades. Moss grew on the red tile roofs of the old colonial buildings. Patios and balconies were aglow with geraniums of every shade from scarlet to palest pink.

Though it was after midday and most shops and businesses were closed for lunch, Indians, whites, mestizos and negroes ebbed and flowed across the streets and plazas like a tide. Smart business suits and floating silks moved alongside cheap cottons and stained, ragged blankets.

'Taxi!' Ross raised his hand and with a squeal of brakes a battered Cadillac with a Mercedes radiator rocked to a halt beside them, the current number one in the Ecuadorian hit parade blaring at full volume from the open window.

The driver squinted up at them through his sunglasses, shifted the wad of chewing gum to the other side of his mouth and, smoothing his Zapatta moustache with finger and thumb, jerked his head as he spoke. Kara couldn't hear a word above the deafening music. Obviously Ross had the same problem for, with a gentle smile, he reached inside the car and flipped off the small transistor lying on the shelf above the dashboard. The sudden silence was shocking.

'Hey,' the driver began aggrievedly, 'what you think you—'

'Do you want a fare?' Ross asked calmly.

'Where you wanna go?' the driver demanded truculently, weighing the possibility of cash against deprivation of noise.

'The northern sector—without music.' Ross named an hotel and Kara looked at him quickly, then remembered he had come to Quito from Colombia. Naturally he would have put up at an hotel before setting out for the clinic.

The driver hesitated and Ross turned away, raising his arm to flag down another cab. 'OK, OK,' the driver capitulated and while Ross opened the back door and threw in the rucksacks and saddle-bags, the driver looked Kara up and down, leered and winked.

She gave him an icy glare that had no effect at all and climbed into the car. She had encountered such behaviour before. In a way it was only to be expected. Though with her colouring she was obviously not Indian or even mestizo, her trousers, poncho and soft felt hat hardly clarified her nationality or her profession.

Moving at what seemed to Kara a highly dangerous speed, they raced through the heart of the city, past the stately cathedral with its wide, shallow steps leading to the grey stone portico, past City Hall, the Archbishop's palace and the President's residence.

'Just how many churches are there in this city?' Ross demanded as they passed yet another.

'Eighty-six.' Kara smiled at his double-take.

'Then they must be the most holy or the most godless people in South America,' Ross remarked drily.

As they reached the northern part of the city, the buildings grew more modern and the roads widened into avenues. The residential suburbs expanded on to a lush plain commanding a magnificent view of the eastern mountains. Kara glimpsed luxurious private houses set in immaculate gardens as they sped by.

The driver pulled up outside the hotel and, the instant Ross had paid him, switched on the transistor and roared off in a cloud of exhaust and noise. Kara pulled off her hat as they entered the lobby and felt a prickle of apprehension at the crowd of business-suited men with cards pinned to their lapels who seemed to fill the reception area.

Ross eased his way to the desk with Kara close behind him, acutely aware of the stares she was attracting. She could not hear what he said above the chattering crowd, but the male receptionist's apologetic shrug and repeated shake of the head were all too plain.

'Fully booked,' Ross said briefly when they were once more outside on the pavement. 'It's a convention of some sort. Do you know any other hotels?'

'I think there's one similar to this on the next avenue, by the park. The only other one I know is Quito's equivalent of the Ritz and that's—'

'Forget the Ritz,' Ross said bluntly, 'this is work, not a holiday.'

'I'm well aware of that,' Kara retorted sharply, stung by his assumption that she would automatically choose the most expensive place. She knew more about penny-pinching than he ever would.

They reached the hotel ten minutes later, only to meet with the same reply, this time from a female receptionist, a large middle-aged woman with gold-rimmed spectacles and an air of regal disdain. In the swift, appraising glance that raked them both, Kara read scorn.

'With great regret, Señor,' she ignored Kara completely, 'there are no rooms available. There is a convention in the city and we have some early tourists.' She gave the slightest shrug.

Kara turned to leave, but instead of following her, Ross leaned forward.

'Perhaps you would be good enough to fetch the manager,' he said mildly, but Kara heard the icy undercurrent and glanced round. His smile was without warmth or humour.

'The manager, Señor?' The receptionist blinked as if such a request were unheard of. 'I assure you, I am quite competent to deal with any—'

'The manager,' Ross was quiet, but adamant as he

placed his UN identification on the desk. 'We are doctors and have urgent business.'

'Ah, doctors,' the receptionist tore her gaze from the identity card and flashed him a blinding smile. 'Forgive me, Señor, I did not realise—'

'Quite,' came Ross's dry comment.

'One moment, I will check again. Yes, I see there was one cancellation. How could I have missed it?'

'How indeed?' Ross murmured.

'Would that suit you and—' the sharp eyes flickered over Kara once more, resting momentarily on her wedding ring.

'It will suit us perfectly,' Ross interrupted, signing the register. He scooped up the key as the woman laid it on the desk. 'I'm sure my wife and I will be very comfortable.' Ross seized Kara's elbow and propelled her swiftly towards the lift. 'Won't we, darling?'

Startled, only just realising what had happened, Kara stiffened.

'The porter will bring your bags, Señor,' the receptionist called after Ross.

'How kind,' he replied over his shoulder.

Kara glared angrily up at him as they entered the lift, followed by the young porter carrying the rucksacks and saddle-bags. She glanced at the porter, who was idly eyeing them both, then hissed at Ross in English, 'I am not sharing a room with you, and that's final.'

'Smile, dear, the porter will think we've quarrelled,' Ross grinned, infuriating Kara even more.

'I don't give a damn what the porter thinks, and let go of my arm, you're hurting me.'

Ross's only reaction was to tighten his grip as the lift clanked to a stop and the doors opened. 'We'll discuss this inside, not here in the passage.'

'There's nothing to discuss,' Kara said breathlessly as she was hustled down the corridor, forced to run to keep up with Ross's long stride.

He opened the door and the porter took the bags in and laid them on the nearest of the twin beds. Ross tipped him as he left, then closed the door and leaned against it, releasing Kara's arm. She snatched it away, rubbing where his fingers had dug into her flesh.

'Before you say another word, show me how much money you've brought with you,' Ross demanded.

Stunned, Kara looked up at him. 'But I haven't any, you know that.'

'Then as I am paying for our accommodation and all our funds are required to restock the clinic and we appear to have a bed each, just what are you in such a lather about?'

Kara turned away, her cheeks burning. How did he always manage to twist things so that his version was the only reasonable one? Put like that her protest sounded ridiculous. But it wasn't. He didn't consult her, he never explained, he just took over

'Well, why did you imply we were married?' she blurted.

'Do you think we'd have got the room if she thought we weren't?' Ross raised a sardonic brow. 'Use some sense. This is South America, strongly Catholic and highly moral. Besides, what about your reputation?'

'What about my reputation?'

'You wouldn't have one left if word got around that you had shared a room with a man not your husband.'

'But that's the whole point,' Kara exploded. 'You're not my husband and I don't want to share a room with you.'

'Well,' Ross said abruptly, 'you've no choice.'

'This is all your fault!' Kara was furious. 'You make far too many assumptions.'

Ross grabbed her shoulders, almost lifting her off the ground. 'So do you. What's the matter with you? You're a grown woman, you've been married. What are you so afraid of?'

'I'm not afraid of anything,' Kara said quickly.

'Oh, really?' Ross glowered. 'Then why are you acting as though I'd engineered this whole situation for sexual purposes?'

Kara flushed painfully. 'I'm not—I didn't—'

Ross's dark brows lifted. 'Can't you see how a man could feel hurt, always being regarded as a sex-fiend?' he demanded solemnly.

Kara stared at him, totally confused, then in the depths of his gaze she saw teasing laughter. It found an echo in her own heart and she relaxed, realising for the first time how tense she had been.

She smiled apologetically. 'Sorry.' She lifted one shoulder in a shy shrug. 'I, er, it's—'

Ross placed a gentle finger on her lips, 'No explanations,' he said softly. 'We'll talk later, when we have more time.' Releasing her he turned to his rucksack, pulling out his notebook and wallet. 'You phone the lawyers and fix an appointment for this afternoon, then take a taxi to collect all the household stuff. I'll get on to the hospital and pick up the drugs and medical supplies.'

Kara stiffened. He was doing it again, taking over, organising. Yesterday she had been happy for him to do it, but today it made her feel threatened and undermined, as though all that she had worked for was being removed from her grasp, placed beyond her control.

Ross glanced up. 'Of course we could swap, you know as much about the medical requirements as I do, but I warn you, I'd make an utter hash of the domestic—'

'No,' Kara laughed, shaking her head. He really could read her thoughts. Overwork must be making her paranoid. He was no threat, he was simply trying to use their limited time efficiently. She picked up the phone and asked for an outside line while Ross checked several lists, laying out papers and money on the bed.

'Mr Medina will see us at four,' Kara announced as she put the phone down.

'Fine, I'll meet you at his office.' Ross was brisk and business-like. 'Here's a bank draft for two hundred dollars. Take it to the central bank and they'll exchange it for local currency. You should get about five thousand sucres. That should cover the domestic supplies. Get receipts so we can keep the bookwork tidy, and here's some cash for a taxi.'

Kara nodded, picked up her own list, folded it with the bank draft and put it in her pocket. As she turned to go Ross caught her hand and thrust five crumpled notes into it, saying brusquely, 'You may need a few things for yourself—stuff not on the lists.'

Kara opened her hand, looked at the money, at Ross, then back at the money. 'But those are hundred sucre notes. That's about twenty pounds,' she said, startled.

Busy scribbling on an official-looking form, Ross shrugged, sounding irritated. 'So, you won't be able to buy up the town.'

'I didn't mean it that way,' Kara said quickly. 'Ross, I—I can't take money from you!'

'Oh, for God's sake,' he sighed in exasperation, 'consider it a loan if it will make you feel better, but get going, will you?'

She hesitated a moment longer. 'Go!' he shouted, pointing at the door.

'Thanks,' Kara murmured, her eyes shining as she stuffed the money into her other pocket. Should she treat herself to some moisturiser? What about some scented soap, or better still, a jar of rich hand cream?

Overwork, lack of time, and the harsh conditions had taken their toll over the past few years. And if she were honest, there had been little incentive to make any extra effort with her appearance. Luis had never noticed, and there had always been more important matters requiring her attention. But now—now was not the time to examine too closely the reasons for her change of heart.

Lost in her thoughts, Kara did not notice the expression on Ross's face as he watched her leave.

The afternoon passed in a flash. Taking a taxi to the principal shopping district of Carrera Guayaquil after cashing the bank draft, Kara made the cab wait while she dashed in and out of the shops. First she bought flour, sugar, margarine, vegetable oil, coffee and rice. The list was long and she added dried fruit, salt, spices, honey, canned fish, seeds, beeswax, two new axes, two soft brushes, dishcloths and preserving jars. Then, toilet soap, toilet paper, disinfectant, liquid detergent, shampoo, toothpaste and toothbrushes, and on to yet another shop for fresh fruit, yoghurt and yeast.

At last it was done, every item ticked off. Breathing a sigh of relief, Kara picked up the final pair of bulging carrier bags and walked down the arcade to where the taxi waited with the rest of her shopping.

Looking forward to the luxury of a proper bath, with creamy, scented soap and matching talc, and wondering whether she should have bought the larger bottle of hair conditioner, Kara glanced sideways into the window of a small, exclusive-looking gown shop, and stopped dead. She ignored the dress in the centre of the window, a confection of tiered black lace, for behind it, displayed with artful simplicity, was the most elegant blouse she had ever seen.

Of finest silk in a soft shade of peach with a high, frilled neckline and full sleeves, it shimmered like dew-spangled gossamer. Kara knew it would suit her to perfection. She looked at the price tag, so discreet as to be almost hidden. Four hundred and fifty sucres. The amount she had intended returning to Ross after buying her personal bits and pieces. If she bought the blouse, it would take every cent of the money he'd given her—loaned her, she corrected herself quickly. She fully intended to pay him back as soon as the legal business was settled.

Oh how she wanted that blouse! Just for once to feel pure silk against her skin instead of serviceable cotton or warm flannelette. But to spend all that money on one garment, something she would wear only rarely, seemed almost wicked. She did have the green and white sprigged cotton, and there wasn't anything wrong with it, except it was so ordinary, so *serviceable*. She had scrimped and saved and gone without for so long, surely she could justify this one extravagance?

Tonight she and Ross would be having dinner together in the hotel. It would be the first time he had seen her in anything other than jeans and a sweater. Tonight was going to be different, special. Tonight she wanted to look like a woman. She pushed open the door.

Kara was late getting back to the hotel and after unloading everything with the help of the driver and the porter, she barely had time to wash her face and hands and smooth back her hair before diving into the taxi once more. Even so, it was after four when she arrived at the lawyer's office.

There was no sign of Ross and nervousness dried Kara's mouth as she realised she would have to face Mr Medina alone.

From behind one of the doors she could hear the sound of men's voices raised in argument. She gave her name to the secretary, but instead of asking her to take a seat, the girl beckoned her forward and knocked on the heavy door leading to an inner office. The voices stopped immediately and the girl opened the door, standing back to let Kara enter.

The first person she saw was Ross, standing by the window. He nodded a curt greeting, then turned away to look down onto the street. The lawyer, seated behind a huge, leather-topped desk, rose to his feet at once, extending his hand.

'Señora Noreno, it is a pleasure to see you once again.' His thin face was finely crinkled like old parchment, and his voice had the same dry quality. But his handshake was firm and the welcome seemed genuinely warm.

Kara made a brief reply, but the atmosphere was almost tangible. What had the two men been arguing about when she arrived?

'Please, do sit down, Señora.' The lawyer gestured to a shiny leather armchair. As she lowered herself into it, Kara darted a glance at Ross, silhouetted against the window, his back to the room.

'Dr Hallam has explained his interest in the situation and has put forward several points for consideration.' Mr Medina leaned back in his swivel chair and steepled his hands, surveying Kara over the tips of his fingers. 'For my part, I have tried to put to him the family's position.'

Tried? Was that what they were arguing about? Kara wondered, but Mr Medina was still talking.

'Taking into account their business commitments, and the interests related to those businesses, they are of course bound to attempt to re-deploy the money Luis left. As you know, I did not draw up Luis's will, and I must confess the matter is somewhat complicated.'

'It seemed perfectly straightforward to me,' Kara broke in. 'It's the family who are complicating—'

'I believe you have found it difficult to accept that there's no personal animosity in this matter, their attitude is simply one of anxiety, to do the best for the greatest number with the finance available.'

Kara's nostrils flared as she heard him utter the same words he had used on the last occasion she had sat in this office, three weeks after Luis's death. She opened her mouth to protest, but he continued talking in the same quiet, precise manner, making her feel gauche and melodramatic and unable to interrupt without seeming appallingly rude.

'Even if the money were released to you,' the lawyer went on, 'at the present rate of inflation, and considering the speed at which it was being used, it would not last many more years. And what would have been achieved at the end of it? The Indians are totally resistant to change. They lack education, insight and any desire to better themselves.'

Kara could take no more. 'I really can't accept that, Mr Medina,' she held her temper tightly under control, bitterly aware that there was a grain of truth in what he said. 'The last time we met you made these same points. They were not a valid reason for withholding the money then and are even less so now. Of course there is resistance to change. Every change to come into the Indians' lives so far has been for the worse. Naturally they are suspicious. But I have seen an enormous difference in their attitude in the last twelve months, and the clinic has been responsible. Not only in combating disease but in other areas of their lives, food production for example.'

'Señora Noreno,' the lawyer cut in gently, 'surely that is outside your scope? A matter for the relevant government department.'

'I couldn't agree more,' Kara said firmly, willing herself to remain calm, reminding herself that he was merely a spokesman for the family, he was not personally involved. 'If the government had shown any interest or organisational ability in tackling the fundamental problems of land distribution and management then my involvement would be totally unnecessary. As it is, I have no choice. It is as much a matter of life and death as the medical side of my work.'

Kara glanced at Ross, but his back was still towards her. Why didn't he say something? Why didn't he add his weight to her argument? He must know she was right, so why wasn't he helping her?

Voices sounded in the outer office. The door opened and a slender, dark-haired man of about forty, wearing an expensive suit, heavy-framed glasses and a beaming smile, walked in.

'My dear Kara, how marvellous to see you.' He took her hand and kissed it. 'It has been far too long since we enjoyed your company.'

That had dragged Ross's attention back into the room, Kara noted wryly. 'Good afternoon, Francisco.' Her greeting was calm and formal, giving no hint of the turmoil within her. Mr Medina must have contacted him right after receiving her phone call. The fact that Francisco had not even greeted the lawyer confirmed Kara's suspicion that they had spoken very recently. Now they would really put the pressure on.

Ross moved easily across to stand behind Kara's chair. One hand remained in his pocket, the other, brushing across her shoulder with momentary pressure before resting casually on the back of the chair, warned her to remain seated.

'Francisco, may I introduce Dr Ross Hallam. He's from the UN and is doing a viability study of the clinic.' Francisco's eyes lit up as he extended his hand. 'Ross, this is Francisco Noreno, Luis's cousin. He looks after the Quito end of the family businesses.'

The two men murmured conventional greetings as they shook hands and Kara was momentarily amused watching them sizing one another up. But the seriousness of the situation soon put everything else out of her mind.

'Dr Hallam,' Francisco was at his most sincere, 'I would like you to understand that, far from wishing to deprive the Indians of anything, it is our earnest desire to help them.'

He's going to try and push the responsibility of the clinic onto the UN, Kara realised with a flash of intuition.

'They need jobs, which our companies can provide. Surely this is of more use than free medicine? I ask you, which will be of greater benefit in the long term?'

'Tell me something, Francisco,' Kara said tightly,

'with seventy-five in every thousand children dying before they reach their second year, and malnutrition and preventable diseases killing thousands more, where is your next generation of labour to come from if you stop their free medicine?'

Francisco smiled broadly. 'Look, this is no way to discuss such important matters.' He opened his arms to include Ross and Kara. 'You must be my guests for dinner tonight so that we may talk in a more relaxed and informal atmosphere. I am sure we can solve this problem in a way that will benefit us all.'

'That sounds like a good idea,' Ross agreed, oblivious to Kara's pleading glance.

'Splendid,' Francisco beamed. 'My aunt will be pleased to receive you, Kara, and our cousin Beatriz is on holiday from Guayaquil. You remember Beatriz?'

'Who could forget her?' Kara murmured with a sinking feeling in the pit of her stomach.

'That is settled then. I will send my car for you at seven-thirty. We dine at eight. At which hotel are you staying?'

Kara told him, and with earnest assurances of the warm welcome awaiting them, Francisco ushered them out of the office.

As they returned to the hotel Kara was very quiet. The sudden change of plans for the evening had disappointed her more than she expected. Yet they could hardly have refused the invitation. To have done so would have been taken as an insult and would have put her in the wrong, making it look as though she were responsible for the delay in settling the will, when in fact the opposite was true.

There had been no alternative, but instead of looking forward to an evening alone with Ross, away from the pressures of the clinic and in neutral surroundings where she could get to know him a little better, Kara could already feel her stomach knotting with tension.

'Not nervous, surely?'

Kara glanced sideways to see Ross watching her, an amused smile lifting the corners of his mouth.

'If you knew the rest of the family, you wouldn't need to ask,' Kara retorted.

'I thought I was aware of all your faults,' Ross reflected, 'and I certainly wouldn't have listed lack of courage among them.'

'Well thanks!' Kara flared. 'You certainly are a master in the art of back-handed compliments.'

'What is it then, have you lost the will to fight?'

'No, I haven't. But if your name was Daniel, would you breeze into the lions' den a second time?'

Ross grinned. 'Like that, was it?'

'Exactly like that,' Kara glared.

He leaned towards her, his eyes glinting. 'But tonight, there'll be two of us. You're not alone any more.' He leaned back against the seat and stretched, then ran his hands through his rumpled hair. 'I've a feeling that tonight is going to be very interesting,' he mused, 'very interesting indeed.'

Kara scarcely heard. Another phrase was echoing in her heart. Not alone any more. Not alone any more.

She was still in the shower when Ross returned from the bathroom down the hall.

'I'm going down for a drink,' he shouted through the door. 'Don't hurry, you've plenty of time.'

Which, roughly translated, means I'll need every second to get myself looking presentable, Kara thought as she worked the creamy shampoo fiercely through her hair. But the luxury of endless hot water, the shampoo's rich lather and the subtle perfume of the soap, quickly soothed away her edginess.

Wrapped in a soft, fluffy towel, with another one around her head, she gave herself a manicure, finishing off with lashings of hand cream. Then, having no varnish, Kara buffed her nails to an opalescent sheen. She rubbed her hair as dry as she could with the towel, completing the task with a hand-dryer loaned by the lady in the next room, one of a party from New Jersey going on to Peru the following day.

Then, smoothing moisturiser into her skin, which still glowed from the shower, Kara darkened her lashes with mascara, applied peach gloss to her lips and began to dress.

Ready at last, she turned to look in the full-length mirror on the wardrobe door. She could hardly believe her eyes. A stranger stared back at her, a slender, elegant stranger.

Her hair fell to her shoulders from a centre parting in a curtain of honey-gold. Her smoky eyes seemed huge in her finely drawn face.

The blouse was perfect, as she had known it would be, its subtle shade matched exactly by her lip-gloss. The filmy material lay against her skin as lightly as a breath. She had hung her skirt in the steam-filled shower for a few minutes and now the fine wool fell in deep folds from the narrow waist-band without a crease. Kara hitched up her skirt and slipped her feet into her shoes, the toes peeping out from the froth of lace on the hem of her petticoat.

The knock on the door made her jump and her cheeks were pink as she turned away from the mirror, feeling oddly guilty at having lavished so much time and attention on herself. 'Come in,' she called, guessing it was Ross.

As he entered, catching his sleeve on the door handle, Kara's heart lurched painfully. Freshly bathed and shaved, his thick black hair as tidy as a comb could get it, he was devastatingly handsome in a cream shirt with cream and brown striped tie, fawn trousers and a bottle-green corduroy jacket. His heavy boots had been replaced by polished brown leather shoes. Freeing his sleeve he looked up, and Kara felt a slow tide of warmth flood through her at the expression that burned in his dark eyes.

Wordlessly he gestured for her to turn round. Kara spun lightly on her toes, her hair and skirt swirling softly about her. He took a step forward and, as she faced him once more, clasped her to him.

'The butterfly has emerged from her chrysalis,' he murmured, and lowered his head to hers.

But as Kara lifted her face, anticipating his kiss, eager to feel the touch of his lips, he hesitated.

'Oh God, it's almost eight,' he groaned, 'and you've got to be in the lobby when the car arrives.'

Kara gasped as she remembered. 'You signed us in under your name and Francisco's driver will ask for Señora Noreno!'

In a confusion of disappointment, embarrassment and irritation, Kara pulled free and snatched up her lacy shawl.

'You see how you've complicated everything?' she cried, running to keep up with Ross as he strode down the corridor to the lift.

He glanced down at her. 'I've a suspicion things are going to get a lot more complicated yet,' he said softly.

CHAPTER FIVE

THE PALE blue Mercedes had a glass panel between the driver and passengers. Ross settled himself beside Kara and the car glided away from the hotel. He indicated the panel.

'Your brother-in-law obviously likes privacy.' He looked about him. 'And a degree of comfort. Fine leather upholstery, seats at least a foot thick and plenty of leg room. That's usually a major problem for me.' His teeth gleamed in the dim light as he grinned at her. 'Unless I'm in the front seat I usually end up with my knees in my mouth.'

Kara smiled. Could he see how nervous she was? Was he trying to ease the tension?

'Tell me about the family,' Ross demanded. 'How many are there? Who lives where? What is the business set-up?'

Kara took a deep breath. 'The Norenos are of mixed Spanish and Italian descent. Overall control of the businesses is in the hands of two brothers, Antonio in Guayaquil and Garcia here in Quito.'

Ross looked puzzled. 'I thought you said Francisco was in charge at this end?'

'He is really. Garcia, Francisco's uncle, has heart disease and is a permanent invalid.'

'Why didn't one of Garcia's own children take over? Why did he have to import a nephew?'

'He only had two,' Kara looked away briefly. 'Luis, who is dead,' she met Ross's gaze once more, 'and Carlotta, who married one of the haciendados down in Riobamba.'

'What exactly are the businesses?'

'Antonio and his elder son, Juan, are in food processing. They have a sugar refinery and manufacture jams, preserves and sweets. That's in the main port. Francisco runs several small textile factories here in Quito.'

'Is Francisco married?'

Kara nodded. 'His wife's father owns one of the private banks here in the capital. They have two sons, both at university, and two daughters who are much younger, about twelve and ten.'

'And who is Beatriz?'

Kara could feel Ross's eyes on her, studying her reaction. He seemed oddly amused. She would give him facts. Anything else he would have to work out for himself, and it was only a matter of minutes before he would have ample opportunity to do just that. 'Beatriz is Juan's daughter, Francisco's niece.'

'How old is she?'

'About twenty-four.'

'Does she work? Not that she would need to,' he added drily.

'She's a designer,' Kara said without expression, 'textiles mostly, but there was a mention of her wanting to branch out into fashion. She's also done a business management course.'

Ross's eyebrows lifted. 'Quite a career girl. You and she must have a lot in common.'

'Oh, no,' Kara returned flatly. 'I suppose at one time it could have been said we had a mutual interest,' Kara's mouth twisted, 'but not now.'

'Where is she based?'

'She divides her time between here and her father's office in Guayaquil,' Kara answered carefully. 'I believe she's being groomed to share the running of the companies with Juan and Francisco when her grandfather retires.'

The car purred to a halt outside wrought-iron gates set

in a high wall which stretched out of sight in either direction. Ross watched the driver press a remote control device. The gates swung open silently. 'He certainly does value his privacy,' Ross repeated.

'I've never been able to decide whether the walls are to keep everyone else out or the family in,' Kara confided with a rush of nervousness. 'This place always reminds me of an opulent, expensive, beautifully furnished cage.'

They swept up the curving drive, through floodlit gardens fringed with palms, lemon trees and jasmine. Masses of flowers edged the immaculate lawns and Kara could not help thinking of the Indians who lived near the clinic, bent double every day as they tried to scratch enough to live on from the barren soil. The contrast was vivid and horrifying.

They drew up outside the sprawling white villa. To the right a large, oval swimming-pool sparkled under the lights.

'What recession?' Ross murmured cynically as he got out of the car, reaching in to help Kara. 'Just one thing,' he said softly as they followed the chauffeur across the terrace to the front door, 'how did you know what was in your husband's will? Did he tell you?'

Kara darted a startled glance at him. 'Yes, of course.'

'Have you actually seen the document?' Ross kept his voice low as the chauffeur knocked on the door.

Kara nodded. 'Yes, once. I couldn't understand it all, my Spanish—'

The door was opened by a uniformed major-domo, who bowed formally and stood back to let them enter.

'How many trustees?' Ross muttered.

'I don't know,' Kara shrugged helplessly. She had never been able to find out all the details. Mr Medina had always been pleasant and polite and appeared helpful, but when it came down to hard facts and detailed information, he had been curiously evasive. Why was it important? What had Ross learned? There was no time to ask.

Francisco, in a wine velvet jacket, ruffled shirt and black trousers, emerged from a doorway and hurried down the wide hall to greet them.

'I welcome you both. *Mi casa es su casa*,' he gave the traditional Spanish welcome—my house is your house—as he kissed Kara's hand, then shook Ross's.

Unease sat on Kara's shoulders like a weight. The last time she had set foot in the villa had been the day of Luis's funeral. That day she had felt a total outcast, accused, rejected and damned.

As she hesitated, Ross slipped his hand under her elbow. A light touch, to the casual observer nothing more than a courteous gesture. But to Kara it was a life line. She was not alone. Her back straightened, her chin rose and, as she took a deep breath, Ross, barely moving his lips, whispered, 'Butterfly.'

A glow radiated outwards from Kara's heart. She smiled at Francisco, noticing for the first time a fine patina of sweat on his face, though to her neither the night nor the house seemed unduly warm. With Ross's protective presence towering beside her, she entered the drawing room.

The murmur of conversation ceased abruptly and Kara, vaguely aware of other people, had no time to notice who they were or how many as Francisco, rubbing his hands together with a nervousness that was quite out of character, led them to where a woman of about sixty, dressed entirely in black, sat stiffly upright on a high-backed chair. Her silver-streaked hair was drawn into a severe bun. Grief had left permanent marks on her thin, aristocratic face so reminiscent of her son's, and her expression was cold, with a trace of bitterness.

Despite the unhappiness Luis's mother had caused, Kara could still feel sorry for her. She had been cast in the matriarchal mould, but with her husband a permanent invalid, the business run by a nephew, her only son dead and her daughter absorbed into another important family, what had she left?

'Good-evening, Dona Elena,' Kara's voice, despite her inner turbulence, was calm and level. She did not commit the error of extending her hand. She knew better now. The first time she had met Luis's mother she had been anxious to please, wanting desperately to be accepted. Though the older woman's manners had been impeccable, contempt and disdain had been loud in her eyes. Now Kara waited for her to make the first move.

The birdlike eyes studied her with sharp intensity. Then a thin, bony hand was proferred. The brief touch reminded Kara of an autumn leaf, weightless, arid and brittle.

'You've changed.' The terse observation encompassed acknowledgment of all the differences between them, acceptance of a fate in which her beloved only son had rejected the life planned for him, only to die in a ghastly accident. And, to Kara's astonishment, it also contained a hint of admiration.

'Yes, Señora,' Kara agreed quietly, 'I have changed. I think maybe we both have.'

Dona Elena inclined her head. The subject was closed. 'And who is this?' She surveyed Ross.

'Señora, may I present Dr Ross Hallam from the United Nations Health and Development Council. Ross, this is Dona Elena Noreno.' Something stopped her as she was about to add, 'My late husband's mother.' Was it that suddenly she no longer felt bound to the family? Such bonds as existed had been legal, rather than ties of genuine affection. Francisco and Carmen had been friendly, but there had been little real depth or warmth in their rare meetings. Or was it that she wanted to leave the past behind, to set aside the weight of sadness and regret and move on? But to what?

As Ross bent over the extended, claw-like hand and, without a trace of awkwardness or self-consciousness, raised it to his lips, the old woman's thin mouth quivered momentarily. 'What a loss to the diplomatic service, Dr Hallam.'

Ross straightened up with an enigmatic smile. 'Señora,' he inclined his head.

'Francisco, I will go upstairs now. Carlos can take me,' Dona Elena announced to her hovering nephew. He beckoned at once to a mop-haired youth. She switched her gaze to Kara. 'Dining late does not suit me. I have a light supper in my room.'

An explanation, or an excuse for not joining them? Which was it, Kara wondered. 'Good-night, Señora,' she said softly. 'I am glad to have seen you.' The strange thing was, it was true. Something had changed. The nervousness and fear inspired by the old woman had gone, and they both knew it.

Dona Elena glanced at Kara, then at Ross, then left the room on the arm of her great-nephew. The major-domo approached with a silver tray.

'Kara, will you have sherry? Or there is madeira if you prefer.' Francisco indicated the fluted crystal glasses.

Kara had sweet sherry, Ross dry. Carlos returned and came over to be introduced, his limpid brown eyes full of adoration as he gazed at Kara. Carmen, Francisco's wife, joined them just as the major-domo announced that Francisco was wanted on the telephone. Señor Medina wished to speak to him on a matter of some urgency.

Kara thought Francisco paled slightly as he excused himself and hurried out. Carmen went on talking in her slow, formal manner.

'Maria and Juanita are in their rooms. They have had their supper, now they are watching TV.' She explained in answer to Kara's enquiry, 'I do not believe it is good for them to be around at dinner parties, especially if business is being discussed. Both sides suffer. Please excuse me for one moment.' She left them as Francisco re-entered the room.

'It certainly wasn't good news,' Ross murmured in Kara's ear as Francisco, deep in thought, his face grey and lined, lifted a glass from the tray, drained it, and with a tiny shudder placed it on a side-table. He strode towards them, rubbing his hands together briskly as he arranged his face in a smile.

'I wonder where Beatriz can be?' he glanced at his watch.

Carlos sniffed loudly as he replaced his glass on the tray. The major-domo deftly whisked it away before he could take another and Kara had to mask a smile at the boy's petulant expression.

She had no doubt that Beatriz was quite deliberately late, but she said nothing.

Then, as if on cue, Beatriz appeared in the doorway, pausing so that all eyes turned towards her. That, Kara was forced to admit, was style, a carefully planned and timed entrance, creating maximum impact.

Everything about Beatriz commanded attention, from her raven hair, swept into an elegant chignon and dressed with two poinsettias the colour of blood, to her high-heeled patent mules. Her dress was of figure-hugging black silk jersey, split to the knee, with a wide, plunging neckline edged with ruffled tiers of crimson chiffon which also formed the cape-like sleeves. Her make-up was flawless. Her apricot skin gleamed and her eyelids, dramatically lined with kohl, glittered with jade, lilac and gold shadow.

Kara felt herself fade almost into invisibility. Her own choice of peach and brown, which had seemed a subtle compliment to her fair colouring, now only looked insipid. It was like comparing a wren with a bird of paradise. Kara kept her head high, but her heart and spirits sank.

Beatriz's delicately arched brows lifted fractionally. 'I do hope I haven't kept you all waiting.' Her mouth was a vivid slash of crimson, moist and pouting.

'Such a vision of loveliness was worth waiting for,' Francisco said immediately, with heavy gallantry containing the merest hint of impatience. Carlos sniffed loudly once more and turned his head away.

'Dinner is served,' the major-domo announced as Beatriz undulated across the room towards them. From the way the material clung without a line or a ridge to mar its smoothness, Kara guessed she wore nothing beneath it.

'But Kara, how pale you are.' Beatriz gripped Kara's shoulders, her long, crimson nails digging lightly into Kara's back as she kissed the air by Kara's cheek. 'And so thin. Have you been ill?'

'How nice to see you again, Beatriz,' Kara said levelly, stepping backward so that the girl was forced to release her. 'No, I've not been ill, just working as usual. But how kind of you to be concerned.'

It was war, there was no doubt about it. Dona Elena might have mellowed, but Beatriz certainly had not.

Kara felt suddenly depressed. None of this was of her making, yet she was caught up in it like a leaf in a gale. The thought of food made her feel ill. How on earth could she eat under these circumstances? But what would Ross say, or do, if she didn't? She glanced up at him. He was looking at Beatriz with a totally unreadable expression.

Kara remembered her social obligations. 'Beatriz, may I introduce Dr Ross Hallam. He—'

Ignoring her completely, Beatriz held out her hand to Ross, flashing him a bewitching smile. 'Ross Hallam,' she repeated his name, rolling it around her mouth, purring it throatily, like a sleek, well-fed cat. 'How marvellous to see you again, and so soon. What brings you back to Quito?'

The words smashed like hammer blows into Kara's heart. They knew each other. They had met before. Yet Ross had asked about Beatriz as if she were a stranger. Why? Why had he pretended?

'I think perhaps we should go in.' Carmen smiled but her eyes were troubled as she watched Beatriz, who had slipped her arm through Ross's and was leading him towards the dining room.

'Please, allow me to escort you,' Carlos offered Kara his arm, the easy courtesy in his manner betrayed by the puppy-like pleading in his gaze.

'How long are you staying?' Beatriz's husky voice floated back to them.

Kara started, looking at Carlos as though she had not understood a word. Then she pulled herself together and put her arm through his. 'Thank you, Carlos, I should like that.'

He flushed scarlet, his wide smile revealing beautiful, even teeth. 'Why do you not visit more often?' he asked. 'That witch,' he flashed a venomous glare at Beatriz who was enrapt in her conversation with Ross, drawing him round the large table to sit beside her, 'she is here too much, but you we hardly ever see.'

Trying to ignore the awful hurt that was welling up in her, Kara forced a smile as she turned to Carlos. 'Why do you refer to your cousin as a witch? She is a very attractive young woman.'

Carlos sniffed once more and Kara realised it was his way of expressing disgust and contempt. 'Attractive? I suppose so,' he grudged, 'but she has no heart, no feelings.' His face darkened. 'She is cold, like an iceberg. She called me a child.' He flushed angrily at what was obviously a recent slight. 'Me, I am a man.'

Kara realised at once what had happened. Carlos was almost nineteen. He had probably attempted a mild flirtation with Beatriz, and she, careless of his pride or his vulnerability, had snubbed him.

'I'm sorry I don't see you more often, but my work is very demanding and I rarely leave the clinic,' Kara explained, not wanting to hurt his feelings more. His face cleared at once and he patted her hand on his arm in a curiously adult gesture, while darting a glance at Beatriz full of childish malice.

Oh no, thought Kara wearily. They reached the table and Carlos pulled out the chair next to his own for her. As Ross and Beatriz were already seated opposite, and Francisco and Carmen had taken their places at either end of the table, Kara had no choice but to accept it.

'Tell me, how are you getting on at university? And your brother, what is he doing? I see he is not here this evening,' she asked, and as Carlos chattered on, ostentatiously ignoring Beatriz while sneaking frequent glances across the table, Kara felt misery overwhelm her. Her face was stiff, set in a polite smile of enquiry as she tried to listen to the torrent of words pouring from Carlos's mouth.

This was not the evening she had imagined, had hoped for. She could not escape from the fact that Ross had lied to her. No, that was not fair, he had not lied. After all he had not said he had never met Beatriz, he had simply allowed her to believe he hadn't.

The soup was brought in and set before them, a maid assisting the major-domo. Kara's stomach revolted, but she gritted her teeth as she unfolded her napkin.

Looking up, she caught Beatriz's eye. An expression of gloating triumph crossed the young woman's face.

Kara remembered Ross's remark about her not lacking courage. Right, she would show him, she would show them all. There were obviously things going on that she knew nothing about. She would put all personal feelings aside. She would think of the Norenos,

Beatriz and even Ross, only in connection with the clinic. Who was for it and who against? Nothing else mattered.

'This soup is delicious, Carmen,' she took a second mouthful. 'It's made from courgettes, isn't it?'

Carmen visibly relaxed, unable to disguise her pleasure at Kara's compliment. 'It is a simple recipe,' she said modestly. 'The courgettes are cooked in a chicken stock, then puréed with cream. I add a little garlic salt and chill the soup before it is served.'

'Carmen does so enjoy the role of housewife,' Beatriz murmured. Then, with an expression of concern which rang totally false, she turned to Kara. 'Are you sure it is not too rich for you? You don't look as though you are used to good food.'

'That just shows how deceptive appearances can be,' Kara replied blandly, 'Almeida looks after me very well.'

'I wouldn't let any dirty Indian touch my food.' Beatriz's shudder had the effect—calculated, Kara guessed—of making the creamy flesh of her half-exposed breasts quiver invitingly. 'Their personal habits are utterly disgusting.'

Tension knotted Kara's stomach as she recognised the opening moves of the battle she now knew was inevitable. 'Almeida is scrupulous about herself, the kitchen and the clinic,' she returned frostily. Beatriz knew full well that Almeida was of mixed blood, but if Kara reminded her of that fact it would look as if she was trying to deny or excuse Almeida's Indian ancestry, and that she refused to do.

'What about you, Ross?' Beatriz's smile was a mixture of challenge and complicity as she pouted up at him. 'Don't you find the whole situation appalling?'

Ross replaced his spoon in the empty dish, apparently quite relaxed as he turned to her with a lazy grin. 'Travelling as much as I do, I've grown used to eating anything put in front of me. But,' he turned to Carmen, 'I must agree with Kara, the soup really is delicious.'

Carmen blushed prettily. 'Please, you must have some more.'

'No,' Ross raised a hand. 'If the rest of the meal is as delightful, I would indeed be foolish to risk spoiling it by over-indulgence, but thank—'

'That's not what I meant,' Beatriz cut in impatiently. 'I'm talking about Kara's obsession with a bunch of lazy, drunken, dishonest Indians, the dregs of society.' The crimson mouth curled as she turned on Kara. 'Are you aiming for sainthood? Are you hoping they'll make a little replica of you to worship?'

'Saint? Me?' Kara was genuinely surprised. 'I've certainly never thought of myself in those terms. Though that is the second time,' she glanced briefly at Ross, who stared back, his expression thoughtful, 'a similar accusation has been levelled at me. If you remember, Beatriz, Luis began the work. I am merely continuing what he started.'

'It killed him,' Beatriz spat, her eyes flashing. 'Are you sure you are not trying to work that off your conscience?'

'Calm yourself, Beatriz,' Francisco tried to placate her as the maid removed the soup bowls and the majordomo brought in a huge platter.

'It is veal, sautéed in butter with a sauce of white wine, paprika and herbs,' Carmen began, looking hopefully at Kara, mild desperation in her smile. Dishes of baby carrots, peas, mushrooms, braised celery and rice were placed on the table.

But Kara could not ignore Beatriz's thrust. 'Actually, my conscience does bother me,' she replied quietly, and was immediately aware of a sudden hush around the table, the silent intake of breath. 'People dispossessed in their own land, suffering from poverty, illiteracy, a high infant mortality rate, low life expectancy, no self-esteem and no chance of improvement—about those things my conscience does bother me. But not about Luis's death. No one could have forseen or prevented that. As for these other things,' a note of briskness entered her voice,' it is not enough to be concerned, I have to try and do something about it, however small.'

'How noble,' Beatriz sneered and Kara remembered, with a pang, Ross's identical reaction. But instead of crushing her, it only strengthened her resolve.

'No,' she said calmly, 'it's not the least bit noble, it's just something that needs to be done.'

'Bravo!' Carlos leaned towards her. 'You have such spirit, such a heart.'

'Eat your meal, Carlos,' Beatriz said as if addressing a recalcitrant child. Carlos flushed angrily but before he could speak, Francisco butted in.

'Surely there are other, better, ways of helping?' He laid down his fork. 'Jobs for instance? If you want to boost a man's self-esteem, you give him a job, not a hand-out.'

'Until the new laws governing the lowest minimum wages were brought in, the Indians were no more than slave labour,' Kara retorted.

'Well, you can't possibly change anything,' Beatriz was scathing. 'You are one woman alone. What can *you* do? You are just throwing Luis's money away. And I am not prepared to sit by and let you do it.'

'Beatriz,' Francisco cut in sharply.

She threw him a look of contempt but remained silent as he smiled ingratiatingly at Kara, then at Ross.

'I was wondering,' he began, toying with his wine glass, 'what are the possibilities of another agency, such as, for example, the one you represent, taking over the clinic?' He beckoned for more wine and the major-domo filled his glass, then moved around the table. Kara shook her head and covered her glass with her fingers. She needed to keep a clear head.

'I believe it is the function of such agencies to give financial assistance where it is required, if requested to do so?' Francisco finished and swallowed half his wine.

Kara knew that she had been right. Francisco was trying to shift the responsibility of the clinic outside the family. She looked at Ross, unconsciously holding her breath as she waited for his reaction.

'That is so,' he agreed easily, 'but such arrangements are usually made between the UN or World Health Organisation and the government of the countries concerned. As this clinic is purely a private venture we are in no way obliged to become involved.'

The food, carefully chosen and beautifully cooked, was like sawdust in Kara's mouth. Even the pineapple meringue, sprinkled with kirsch and topped with cherries, which normally would have delighted her, left her completely unmoved. How could she force another mouthful past her lips? What was Ross up to? Why this cat and mouse game?

'What I don't understand,' he went on calmly, 'is if the clinic was set up and financed privately why the arrangements can no longer continue.'

'But Ross,' Beatriz purred, 'surely you must see that the money is just being wasted?'

'I have visited the clinic,' Ross countered mildly, 'and I saw no signs of waste. Besides, if the money was left to Señora Noreno,' he glanced at Kara who unaccountably blushed, 'to continue running the clinic, which she is obviously trying to do, then I can see no legal way to prevent her.'

Francisco swallowed noisily. 'I hope you do not imply we are doing anything illegal, Dr Hallam?' But he sounded more nervous than accusatory.

'I am a guest in your house, Señor, such behaviour

would be intolerable,' Ross replied with a touch of asperity.

He finished the last of his meringue, placing the silver spoon and fork together on the dish. 'I gather the money has to be administered by trustees, is that correct?'

Francisco settled his glasses more firmly on his nose and shifted in his seat. 'Yes,' he said briefly.

The eyes of Carmen, Beatriz, Carlos and Kara flicked from one to the other of the two men, like spectators at a tennis match.

Ross nodded. 'I believe your factories have recently been under investigation by the government over contravention of the minimum wages laws?'

Kara shivered. Ross's enquiring smile was as friendly as a piranha's.

Francisco's eyes widened. 'How?' He recovered instantly. 'A misunderstanding, a clerical error, nothing more. Of no significance at all.'

'And production levels are down while costs have risen?'

Francisco shrugged, his confidence returning. 'This has happened all over South America. The recession—'

'Who are the trustees?'

Francisco looked momentarily bewildered, but Kara recognised Ross's method of getting at the truth. Hadn't he used that same technique on her only the previous day?

'Er,' Francisco cleared his throat, 'Jaime Medina and myself.'

'Hardly unbiased administrators,' Ross observed with deceptive mildness. 'One hesitates to use words like "conspiracy to defraud."'

Carmen cleared her throat timidly. 'Shall we have coffee?'

'Let's have it in the other room,' Beatriz pushed back her chair. 'This business talk has gone on long enough. Ross,' her voice was honeyed and her eyes heavy-lidded and seductive as she caught his arm, linking her hands around it as he stood up, 'come and tell me about your travels. You must have visited some fascinating places. Have you been to New York? I was there two years ago.' And with a meaningful glance at Francisco, which no one but Kara seemed to notice, Beatriz led Ross out of the dining room.

Kara put down her coffee-cup with fingers that trembled slightly, the scalding, aromatic liquid barely touched.

Beatriz had switched on the stereo and was dancing with Ross, if that slow, sinuous swaying could be called dancing. It had not been his idea, Kara conceded, trying to be fair. Beatriz had dragged him from his seat. It would have been difficult for him to refuse. Beatriz was obviously expert at getting anything she wanted, and all the signs were that she wanted Ross.

Francisco and Carmen were involved in a quiet but intense discussion on the pale leather sofa. They both looked ill at ease, with their fixed smiles and rigid poses.

'What? I'm sorry,' Kara dragged her attention back to Carlos, who was leaning over her chair, insistent and persuasive. 'I'm sure you're a wonderful dancer, Carlos,' she smiled to soften the rejection, 'but I really don't feel like it just now.'

'What's the matter? Is it that bitch? Has she upset you? Is it him?' Carlos jerked his head at Ross. 'I can make you forget him. Dance with me, I can make you forget everything. We'll show them.'

Kara shook her head. 'You're very sweet, Carlos.' She forced lightness into her tone, 'You are my favourite nephew-in-law, but I have a slight headache. I think it would be best if I go back to the hotel.'

'It is her, I know it is. I told you she was a—'

Kara stood up. 'Don't be silly, Carlos,' she said sharply, then made a valiant effort to smile. 'Have you forgotten? I'm a working girl. I need my sleep.' She crossed to where Ross and Beatriz moved lazily to the soulful voice of Julio Iglesias. They turned to look at her, Beatriz smiling, triumph and mockery glittering in her eyes, her golden arms still clasped around Ross's neck.

Kara felt totally excluded. Ross's expression was unreadable. He merely waited for Kara to speak.

'I—it's been a very long day and we've another early start tomorrow, so I think I'll go back to the hotel now.' Come with me Ross. Please want to come with me, her heart pleaded. Don't let me leave alone.

'Yes, you do look tired,' Beatriz agreed immediately, making no effort to sound sympathetic. 'Francisco,' she called over Ross's shoulder, 'Kara wants to go, will you call the car?'

Francisco leapt to his feet, signalling the major-domo. Then he came over to join them. 'I do hope you are not ill?' He at least made some attempt at concern.

'No, it's just a slight headache,' Kara lifted one shoulder apologetically. 'The last few days have been rather hectic.'

'Of course, I do understand.' Francisco placed Kara's shawl over her shoulders.

'Would you like me to come with you?' Ross asked. Beatriz had not relinquished her hold and Ross's hands were still on her waist.

Pride stiffened Kara's spine. 'There is no need. I've no wish to spoil your evening.'

'Of course not,' Francisco took her arm and led her towards the door where Carlos and Carmen joined them.

'I hope you feel better tomorrow,' Carmen said, plainly uneasy.

'Thank you for a lovely meal,' Kara managed, 'it really was delicious. And please give my regards to Dona Elena.'

'I will remember,' Carmen promised.

'Let me ride with you,' Carlos demanded eagerly, 'I will see you safely to your hotel.'

'No, no thank you.' Kara's reply was instant and unequivocal. Carlos was a typical young Latin-American, and Kara knew his pride would demand he made a pass at her. That was more than she could stand tonight.

'The car is outside,' the major-domo announced and before Kara realised what was happening she had been politely but expertly hurried from the house. Within moments the final goodbyes had been said and she was alone in the vast, opulent emptiness of the Mercedes, speeding back towards the hotel.

Her last glimpse of Ross had revealed Beatriz's crimson-taloned fingers pulling his dark head down towards her own, her head thrown back and her body plastered against his so that from breast to ankle not one millimetre of space was visible between them.

Kara sat unmoving during the drive, too numb to think or even to feel. The chauffeur insisted upon accompanying her into reception, saluting politely and turning away once the dragon-like receptionist, impressed despite her habitual disdain, had given her the room key. Kara was relieved she had remembered the number and so avoided mentioning names.

'Your husband is not with you?' The woman could not hide her curiosity.

'My husband—?' Kara was startled but recovered instantly. 'Oh, yes—no, he's been delayed. I'm not quite sure how long he'll be.' She hurried away and crossed to the lift. Delayed in the arms of another woman—but he wasn't her husband.

'Senora Hallam, Senora Hallam!'

Kara's heart gave a thump that left her breathless as she realised the woman was calling her. She turned slowly. 'Yes?'

'Do you wish an early call?'

'Yes,' Kara said decisively, 'for six a.m. please.' The sooner she got away from the city and back to the clinic the better. That was her world. She was needed there. She would immerse herself in work. There would be no time to think of herself, to suffer like this.

She closed the bedroom door, automatically turning the key, and wearily dropped her shawl on the bed. Catching sight of herself in the mirror she was filled with a wild, unreasoning anger. Tearing off her skirt and the delicate peach blouse she hurled them onto the bed and kicked her shoes to the other side of the room. What a fool she had been. What a blind, stupid fool to have imagined Ross Hallam felt anything special for her. Why on earth should he? He had simply been kind and she had built up her hopes for the evening out of all proportion.

In bra and petticoat she prowled the room like a caged animal, restlessly picking things up and putting them down again. Aware of a worsening pain in her breast she hugged herself, trying to contain the anguish that wrenched at the very core of her being.

Ross had called her a butterfly. How wrong he was. She was no butterfly, she was just a plain, dull little moth who had flown too close to the flame and got her wings singed. Beatriz was the butterfly; bright, beautiful Beatriz. Beatriz and Ross together. Oh God, it hurt, why did it hurt so? Kara cried silently. Why couldn't it be me? Why not me in his arms? Why not me held so close?

She stopped her pacing, stunned as she recognised the truth, the cause of her pain. She was jealous. That meant—Kara gritted her teeth. Just how much did she feel for Ross Hallam?

Her mind flew back over all that had happened since she had walked into her sitting room and so unexpected-ly found him there. His arrogant determination to find out the truth for himself, his unexpected gentleness when she broke down, the way he had forced her to eat, his generous help with the patients, acting as her assistant without a thought to pride or seniority; his impatience, his wicked teasing, the flashes of intuition when he seemed able to read her thoughts, the thrill of his touch; his kisses, so rare and unexpected, that seared like flame and transported her into another dimension . . .

You are not alone, he had said, and it had been true. For the first time in her life she had known what it was to be part of another human being. She had not known it with her parents, nor with Luis. But with this stranger, this man she barely knew, the bond was there.

Kara groaned and sank down on the bed, hunched over, her head in her hands. She was deeply, hopelessly in love with Ross Hallam.

No. She snapped upright. It wasn't true. It was just reaction to the loneliness and strain of the past years. Ross Hallam had appeared at a time when, facing severe financial problems, she needed support and was emotionally vulnerable. There was nothing more to it than that. She would get over it. Now she recognised the real truth of the matter she could deal with it.

She got wearily to her feet and, shaking out the crumpled skirt and blouse, folded them neatly. Then she retrieved her shoes and packed them in the rucksack. After washing her face, cleaning her teeth and brushing her hair, Kara pulled on her cotton nightdress, climbed into bed and switched off the light.

She did not love Ross Hallam, it was simply a figment of her imagination. She would rationalise it away. It would soon be gone, and so would he. Scalding tears filled her eyes and, turning her face into the pillow, Kara sobbed herself into oblivion.

Insistent knocking dragged her from a restless sleep. Barely conscious, Kara switched on the light between the beds and stumbled to the door. 'Who is it?'

'Ross,' came the reply. 'Will you open the door or do I wake the night porter for the pass key?'

Fully awake now, Kara hastily unlocked the door and Ross strode in, obviously furious.

'I'm sorry,' she said at once, pushing her hair out of her eyes. 'That wasn't intentional. I locked it without thinking when I got back and forgot to unlock it again before I went to sleep.'

'I see,' Ross took off his jacket, flung it on his bed and began loosening his tie, every movement tight with barely controlled anger.

Kara shivered and it wasn't only from cold. Then it dawned on her that she was standing in front of Ross, naked but for a thin nightdress, while he unbuttoned his shirt and pulled it from the waistband of his trousers, revealing a broad, muscular chest covered with dark, curling hair that spread down over his flat stomach.

She flushed hotly and turned away at once to jump back under the rumpled bedclothes. Ross's hand shot out and grasped her upper arm, holding her back.

'What's the matter?' he frowned. 'Your eyes are swollen.'

'Nothing,' Kara said quickly, lowering her head so that her hair swung forward.

'Don't you take me for a fool as well,' he grated. 'It's plain that something's—' He looked at her closely. 'You've been crying.'

'Of course I haven't,' Kara retorted with as much conviction as she could muster. 'I was in a deep sleep, you woke me up. I've arranged for a six a.m. call,' she changed the subject, trying to be off-hand, 'if you are coming back with me, that is. If you aren't you'll be able to lie in.'

Ross's anger was momentarily overcome by bewilderment. 'If I'm? What are you talking about? Of course I'm coming back.'

As Kara struggled with the conflicting emotions his

answer roused in her, Ross pulled her round towards him, his strong fingers gripping her shoulders, burning into her skin as though the thin cotton were not there.

'Kara, about this evening—'

'No!' she cried, her hands flew up and she gave a mighty push against his bare chest. Surprise loosened his grasp and she pulled free. 'Don't say anything,' she blurted, 'I don't want to know.'

His brows met in a dark line and he held out both hands. 'Look, there's been a mistake.'

Yes, and I made it, Kara grieved silently. 'No,' she backed away, trembling, shaking her head vigorously, her arms clasped tightly across her breasts. 'Please, no more, not tonight. You don't owe me any explanations. I'm—I'm tired, I want to sleep.'

Ross shrugged. 'All right,' he snapped, 'sleep if you must.'

Kara dived into her bed and pulled the covers up to her neck. In two strides Ross was leaning over her, supporting himself with an arm either side of her face, his shirt flapping loosely. She froze, hardly daring to breathe as she looked up at him.

'Sooner or later you are going to have to face certain realities,' he glared down at her, his eyes dark and implacable, his expression steely. 'We have a lot to discuss, you and I, and you can't . . . Oh, damn it!' he exploded softly and, leaning down, his mouth covered hers in a swift, brutal kiss. He flicked the light off and the next instant he had gone.

Her heart hammering furiously, Kara waited, hearing the whisper of clothes as he finished undressing. If he came back what would she do? Hysterical laughter rose in her throat. She could hardly scream, they were supposed to be married.

Then the other bed creaked. 'Good-night Kara,' he growled.

Relieved, disappointed, emotionally exhausted, Kara closed her eyes. 'Good-night, Ross,' she murmured back.

CHAPTER SIX

THE JOURNEY back took ten hours. Ross and Kara, rucksacks bulging, led the mules. Plodding patiently up the steep, rough paths, almost buried under their burden of boxes and packages, the animals also dragged crude sledges loaded with hay and horse-beans. Conversation was minimal. Kara tried to convince herself it was to conserve breath and energy, but both were deeply immersed in their own thoughts, which raised a far more effective barrier than the rugged terrain.

As evening approached and they clattered over the bridge below the clinic, Almeida, resembling a small galleon under full sail, rushed to meet them.

'Señor, Señora,' she panted, relief nudging worry aside on her brown face, 'thank God and all the saints you come! Such trouble—never have I seen—I put them in stable, I did not know what else to do, she no come inside, no touch food I offer—'

'Wait, wait.' Kara laid a calming arm round Almeida's heaving shoulders, 'Just slow down and explain. Who is in the stable?'

'Those poor children and their mother,' Almeida grabbed Kara's hand and hauled her towards the small stone building. 'Come quick, I show you.'

Ross handed the reins of both mules to Vicente who led them away to the kitchen door.

Sprawled in the straw in the abandoned sleep of complete exhaustion, lay a young Indian woman. Two children huddled close to her, their eyes closed, their breathing loud and laboured, each lungful of air a rasping effort.

Kara touched the woman's shoulder and she jerked

upright, her eyes wide open but dull with weariness. All three were dirty and barefoot, their clothes little more than rags.

'You the doctor lady?' the woman gabbled in Quechua. 'You help my sons? We have come over the mountain. My husband, he say brujo will be angry. But you made better my sister's baby last winter. Now you make better my sons. Please, they not die, you not let them die,' she implored.

Kara gently turned the smaller of the two over. At once he began to cough, his feverish little body jerking spasmodically. The rash that covered his face and neck looked black in the dim light.

Ross knelt beside her, watched as she carefully lifted the boy's encrusted eyelid, revealing a bloodshot eye. Then, as Kara checked the child's pulse, he quickly felt with gentle fingers under the boy's chin and round the back of his neck.

Their eyes met. 'It looks like measles,' Kara said quietly, 'except the rash is so dark.'

'It *is* measles,' Ross cut in. 'The colour of the rash is due to blood under the skin. There's obviously some inflammation of the trachea.'

The mother, who had been anxiously watching them both, tugged at Kara's hand. 'You make them well?' She gestured at the rash on the face of the child nearest her.

Kara took a deep breath. The woman's faith in her ability was touching, but the children were obviously desperately ill. 'We'll do everything we can,' she promised. 'Almeida will fetch you something to eat and drink.' Almeida bustled away, patently relieved at having handed over responsibility.

'Did your husband come with you? Is he waiting outside somewhere?' Ross asked, helping the woman to her feet.

She shook her head. 'He went away to find brujo. While he gone, I take children, bring them here.'

'But how?' Kara asked, 'Do you have a mule?'

The woman shook her head again. 'I walk. I carry them. One on back, one—' she made a rocking motion with her arms.

Ross and Kara bent down and, disentangling them from the strips of filthy blanket which the mother had used as a sling, lifted a child each. Their eyes met again. Concern for the children had lowered her guard and Kara was totally unprepared for the sudden lurching awareness that blazed through her, tingling every nerve. In that one brief look, all pretence, all evasion, was stripped from her and she knew it was useless to lie to herself any longer. She could not rationalise it away, now or ever. She loved him, completely and irrevocably.

The children, sensing a stranger's arms about them began to cry, a high-pitched bleating with little strength, which turned to a rasping cough. Ross gestured for Kara to precede him and murmuring soothing words in Quechua, they carried the children into the kitchen.

As they went through to the ward, Kara called to Almeida over her shoulder. 'As soon as you've taken that food to the mother, bring hot water and soap. There's a cake in my rucksack if you can't find the new box.'

The children lay on the thin kapok mattresses, coughing and restless, while Ross lit the lamps, then the fire, and Kara fetched sheets and towels from the linen cupboard.

'If you and Almeida sponge them down, I'll start the generator and get IV sets prepared. Have you any camphorated oil?' Ross straightened up as the flames flickered brightly, throwing a cheerful glow into the room.

'Yes, it's on the second shelf. But why IV sets?'

'They're obviously undernourished and, from the look of them, dehydrated as well. We'll be damn lucky if tracheitis is the only complication and I want some fluids into them as soon as possible.' He disappeared into the theatre.

Thank God he was here. Had she been alone she would have coped but it would have taken far longer. His presence was proving a double-edged sword, invaluable, yet a terrible threat.

Almeida waddled in carrying a huge pan of hot water which she poured into two basins. 'The mother stay outside,' she announced, putting the pan down with a firmness that revealed her exasperation.

'Did you tell her she could come in?' Kara sat down on the edge of the bed and began to undress the youngest boy.

'Si, Señora,' Almeida nodded briskly. 'Come in, I say, see your children, see how the doctors care for them, but she say no.' Almeida shook her head. 'I no understand such a one.' She sat on the other bed and gently eased the older boy forward to remove his ragged shirt. The boy protested feebly, trying to push Almeida's hands away. She clucked her tongue at him. 'What's this? You are not scared of water? A big boy like you? Look at your brother, he not fighting. It will feel so good to be cool and clean. You will see. Come, my little hero, the doctors are going to make you strong and well again.'

Gradually the boy relaxed and Almeida deftly stripped off all his stinking rags and laid a fresh blanket over the skinny, shivering little body.

As Ross opened the ward door from the operating-theatre, Kara could hear the steady thump of the generator. 'She's gone,' he announced briefly.

'Gone? Where?' Kara was stunned.

Ross shrugged. 'Back to her husband, I suppose. The empty plate and cup were by the back door, so at least she won't starve.'

'But the children,' Kara glanced up at him, pausing for a moment in bathing the crusted eyelids of the youngest boy. 'How could she leave them?'

'She knows they're in safe hands and there's nothing more she can do,' he was abrupt. 'She also knows her husband will beat her black and blue for having defied him and the brujo to bring them here. I suppose the longer she's away, the greater her punishment.'

Kara recalled the woman's young-old face, haggard and grimy, her ragged clothing stiff with dirt and grease, her scarred and calloused feet. 'She carried these children for two days,' she murmured.

'Then it will only take her half as long to get back,' Ross replied brusquely. 'Now, are you nearly finished?' He met her quick, angry glare levelly, and she realised his attitude was a deliberate and calculated warning not to allow the emotional side of the situation to overpower her.

'Just a few minutes more,' she answered calmly. She could cope with the boys, but as far as he was concerned, the warning not to allow her feelings to get out of hand had come far too late.

Ross went back into the theatre and as she and Almeida blanket-bathed the boys, sponging them with tepid water in an effort to bring down their temperature, Kara could hear the chink of glass and clatter of metal as he loaded the steriliser. Clean at last, dressed in hospital gowns several sizes too big and tucked between fresh sheets, both children seemed less fearful, but were restless and obviously in pain.

'You see? Wasn't I right? Isn't that better?' Almeida demanded as she squeezed between the beds, clearing up the debris.

Propped up on pillows to ease their breathing, the children followed her movements as she waddled out laden with clothes, towels and the bucket.

Ross came in with the sets and containers of fluid.

'Is that dextrose and saline?' Kara asked.

Ross nodded. 'Have you checked their pulse, respiration and temperature again?

'Just doing it now,' Kara replied, releasing the older boy's wrist onto the sheet and making a note on the chart. How many pairs of hands did he think she had? She hooked the chart over the foot of the bed and putting in the earpieces of her stethoscope, she listened intently, moving the metal disc over the younger boy's chest. He whimpered and coughed.

Kara glanced up, her momentary irritation forgotten. 'Ross, I'm afraid—'

'Broncho-pneumonia?' he interrupted. She nodded, and made room for him. Ross listened to the older boy's chest, then eased him forward to listen to his back. The child's breath was coming in quick, painful gasps. Ross laid him gently back on the pillows.

'Get them connected up to the IV sets,' he said quietly.

'They need antibiotics and something to bring the fever down,' Kara said, her forehead creased in a worried frown.

'They can have soluble aspirin in fruit juice by mouth to start with,' Ross replied, passing the bottle of camphorated oil to her. 'I couldn't get any ampicillin or amoxycillin so I'm going to give them Floxapen via the drip tubing.'

Kara nodded. 'You're right, of course,' and placing the camphorated oil on the trolley she snapped on a pair of sterile gloves and swiftly prepared each boy's arm for the drip.

Once the flow was adjusted and the drug had been injected, Kara gently rubbed each boy's throat and upper chest with camphorated oil, then covered it with a warm pad of wool. Ross checked their pulse and temperature once more and coaxed them both into swallowing the fruit juice containing dissolved aspirin.

Almeida poked her head around the door. 'You want I do anything?'

'Yes, bring a large pan of water to put on this fire,' Ross answered.

'But this small room, he will be full of steam,' Almeida protested.

'Which is exactly what the boys need to help them breathe more easily,' Ross explained patiently.

Almeida's head disappeared. Ross stood up and stretched, then went into the theatre, returning moments later with the oxygen cylinder and mask. 'Just to be on the safe side.' His mouth twisted in a small lop-sided smile. He yawned, then waved at the dressing trolley cluttered with bowls of water, opened packages, dirty gloves and syringes. 'Will you see to this lot?' With that he disappeared into the kitchen. Irritation flared in Kara but she swallowed it down, reminding herself how much more difficult it all would have been without him.

When she returned to the kitchen she left Almeida sitting with the boys, watching and listening for any change in their condition as she gently dabbed their spots with calomine lotion and gave them frequent sips of hot lemon and honey. Ross was standing at the table, snipping the ends off vitamin capsules and squeezing their contents into a glass measure containing about a pink of milky fluid.

He was totally absorbed in what he was doing, a lock of his thick, black hair falling over his forehead, his brows knitted in a frown of concentration. Kara's heart swelled with a surge of love that threatened to suffocate her. It left her legs weak and an ache in the pit of her stomach. She fought to suppress it. Not only was the time he would have to leave drawing closer day by day, but his reaction to Beatriz made it plain he felt no commitment to anyone person. It was hopeless. Why did she persist in torturing herself?

Ross glanced up, caught her eye and said easily, 'Come and see my witch's brew. I've known this work wonders in a matter of days.'

Kara approached the table, her cheeks hot, praying his ability to read her thoughts had momentarily deserted him.

'It's a mixture of goat's milk, vegetable oil and glucose. I'm adding fish liver oil for vitamins A and D.' He snipped another capsule and squeezed it into the bowl, discarding the gelatine shell. 'Can you find the vitamin C powder? It should be somewhere in that pile.' Ross pointed to the stack of boxes Vicente had piled by the cupboard. 'I also got some iron tablets, get those out too, will you?'

He spooned vitamin C powder into the bowl, then wrote down the amount, adding it to the list on his notepad.

Kara folded the iron tablets in a piece of paper and rolled a heavy jar over them, reducing them to a fine powder. She poured it into the bowl and Ross stirred it in, then poured the mixture into two mugs.

'Come on, we'll take one each,' Ross started for the door.

'I think we'll have problems,' Kara said as she eyed the gruel-like fluid, then sniffed it, pulling a wry face. 'They won't care how much good it will do them—if it tastes nasty, they won't drink it.'

'Got any suggestions?' Ross demanded irritably.

'Didn't we have concentrated orange juice on the list?' Kara put the mug down and walked round to the pile of boxes, lifting them down to look at each label. 'Here we are.' She ripped open the box and pulled out a bottle. 'A dollop of this in each mug will make all the difference.' She unscrewed the top then glanced at him, her brows arched in unspoken query.

'Go ahead,' he shrugged, and she poured juice into each mug.

As they walked into the ward Kara said, 'What's going to happen about those drugs you couldn't get? We really do need them.'

Almeida moved out of their way, taking the bottle of calomine to the trolley and throwing the cotton wool pad onto the fire. The water in the pan was boiling and steam wafted into the room.

'I've left an order and the pharmacist has promised to send them up by messenger as soon as he gets new supplies in a day or two.'

With a little coaxing both boys finished every drop of the fortified milk and lay back on the pillows, heavy-eyed and sleepy, the dark rash almost obscured by pink patches of dried calomine. Automatically Kara checked their pulse and temperatures once more. Though their breathing was still quick and raspy, already they seemed in less pain.

Almeida waddled in. 'You come, supper ready.'

It dawned on Kara that neither she nor Ross had eaten since their snack lunch, swallowed as they walked. She glanced at her watch. They had been back at the clinic well over an hour, yet they had been so busy it seemed like only minutes. Replacing the charts, Kara flexed her shoulders, feeling tiredness like a weight on the back of her neck. 'I'd better unpack the drugs first.'

'That can wait until the morning.' Ross pulled the stethoscope from his neck and laid it on the trolley, 'Come on.'

'But—'

'No buts, Almeida will keep an eye on the children.'

'Si, Señora,' Almeida nodded vigorously, 'I stay, and when he finish outside, Vicente come and—' even as she spoke, her husband, carrying the mules' harness, a rag and a battered can of grease, edged round the door.

Kara eyed the leather uncertainly.

'The children, they see me work maybe like their parents do at home, all in same room, they sleep easier.'

It was the longest speech Kara had ever heard from Vicente. His gravelly voice held little expression but he clutched the grease tin with quiet determination.

Kara marvelled at the taciturn man's awareness of the children's fear and distress at the strange situation into which they had suddenly been thrust. 'I think that's a great idea, Vicente,' she said with a smile. 'I'm sure it will help. I'll see you both later,' and with a reassuring smile at the boys, who blinked sleepily back at her, she went out into the kitchen.

Ross had already pushed all the boxes to one end of the table and was ladling out stew onto two plates. Kara sat down opposite him, the glow from the fire warming the side of her face. She picked up her fork with a sudden, vivid memory of the previous evening's meal at Francisco's.

'Nice to be home, isn't it?'

Kara looked up quickly, startled as much by his choice of word—he hadn't said 'back' he'd said 'home'—as by his intuitive awareness of her thoughts. He was watching her, his expression giving nothing away. He took a mouthful. 'Delicious. I'm certainly ready for this. Come on, get started,' he waved his fork at her, 'you didn't eat a lot last night, and you've had very little today.'

'I wouldn't have thought you had time to notice,' Kara retorted and could have bitten her tongue off. The heat in her face now owed nothing to the fire.

'Why should you think that?' Ross's tone was light, but his eyes demanded an answer.

Kara shrugged. 'You and Beatriz obviously had a lot to catch up on. Strange, you never mentioned knowing her when we were talking about the family.' Did it sound as off-hand as she so desperately wanted it to? She wanted him to realise she knew he'd lied, but he mustn't know she cared.

Ross went on eating. 'That's because I didn't know her.' Kara stiffened. 'I mean, I didn't know who she was. The only time I had seen her before was in the adminis-trator's office at the hospital when I first arrived in Quito. I had gone in to make enquiries about this clinic.

She had accompanied her aunt who was at the hospital for X-rays and a consultation about a possible hip-replacement, or so I learned later. Being of an important local family, as well as an extremely attractive young woman,' a pang pierced Kara's heart, and was determinedly ignored, 'the administrator was entertaining her to coffee when I arrived. Seeing he was engaged, I went to talk to his assistant. My encounter with Beatriz Noreno must have lasted all of ten seconds.'

Needing time to grasp not only what he'd said, but all that it meant, Kara pushed her chair back. 'Would you like some water?' She didn't look at him, busy taking tumblers from the cupboard.

'No,' Ross's voice stopped her in her tracks. 'I've got something far more suited to the occasion.'

She swung round as from his rucksack he produced a bottle of wine and flourished it with a grin.

'Oh, I haven't got any wine glasses,' she stammered.

'Who cares? We're eating in the kitchen, off a bare wooden table, in our working clothes. The tumblers are just right,' and as Kara put them on the table he broke the seal, uncorked the bottle and poured the pale amber liquid into each one, filling it three-quarters full.

Kara sat down again and Ross, towering over the table, pushed one glass towards her, raising the other. 'Your good health,' he gave a courtly bow.

'And yours,' the reply was automatic, then she smiled shyly, her mind racing as she lifted her glass. Ross touched it with his own, the soft clink barely audible above the crackling flames. 'What occasion?' she asked, bewildered.

Ross sat down again and picked up his fork. 'Whatever you like,' he lifted one broad shoulder. 'You're glad to be back here, so we can celebrate that, or the fact that I didn't lie to you . . .'

The words hung, echoing in the air.

Kara looked down at her plate. Had it really been so

obvious? She had tried so hard to cover her shock, the hurt.

'You looked like a wounded fawn,' Ross said quietly, sipping his wine, watching her over the rim of his glass.

Kara's head snapped up. 'No.' The involuntary cry revealed an agony of embarrassment and self-contempt. She picked up her fork, toying with the food. 'You must be mistaken. I admit I was rather surprised at the warmth of Beatriz's welcome, especially as I believed you had never met, but—'

'Don't,' Ross warned. 'In the short time we've known one another you've always been honest with me. Painfully so,' he grimaced, and Kara flushed even redder as she recalled their first evening. 'Don't change, don't become like all the rest,' his voice hardened.

Like all what rest? Kara wondered fleetingly. Who had lied to him? About what?

'Well, whatever I looked like,' she mumbled awkwardly, 'I think you misinterpreted. After all, your attention was rather monopolised.'

'Wasn't it just,' Ross agreed drily, finishing the last of his stew. He eased his chair back, stretched his legs out towards the fire and, taking another mouthful of wine, he glanced across at Kara. 'I was being carefully and expertly set up.'

'What?' Startled, Kara almost choked on the potato she was eating.

'Even I, sceptic that I am, didn't realise it at first. That was why I was so angry when I got back to the hotel.'

Kara took a drink. 'I thought you were mad with me for locking the door.'

'That didn't exactly help matters, especially as I believed I had already made it clear that our sharing the room did not require you to share my bed.'

Gripping the tumbler tightly, Kara swallowed some more wine, remembering his swift, brutal kiss and her own tormented emotions when he had abruptly turned away and gone to his own bed, leaving her achingly alone. She was growing more and more confused.

'But I thought you went along with it all, sitting beside her at dinner, dancing so close, staying on after . . .' She broke off quickly. What was she doing? Wasn't she revealing as plainly as if she told him straight out, that his attentions to Beatriz had hurt?

'I had to find out what was behind it all.'

'And did you?'

He nodded, and leaning forward poured more wine into both glasses. Kara was so absorbed by the unfolding story she didn't think of stopping him. 'Francisco's reactions to my shots in the dark about the state of his businesses and the involvement of the law, proved you were right. You guessed he had financial problems.'

Kara felt ridiculously pleased, then chided herself for over-reacting to a few words of praise.

'But when Beatriz kept jumping in to draw my attention away from Francisco, I began to suspect they might have arranged something between them.'

Kara stared at him. 'And had they?' He nodded. She pushed her plate aside. Leaning both arms on the table, Kara clutched her glass. 'What was it?'

He studied her for a moment. 'I was to be persuaded to close down the clinic using whatever reasons or grounds I saw fit.'

Kara was stunned. All the time Francisco had been playing the charming host, he had been plotting to destroy not only the years of work that she and Luis had put in, but the only hope of medical care the Indians had. Carmen must have known what was going on. Was that what they had been arguing about on the settee?

'I did warn you that sooner or later you would have to face certain realities,' Ross said with a grim smile.

'But I thought you meant—' Kara broke off. 'Go on please.'

'Once Beatriz realised I wasn't very receptive to that

idea, she changed her tactics and hinted that another possible solution would be for the UN to take over the clinic.'

'Yes, Francisco mentioned that at dinner.'

'Ah, but Beatriz's plan went a little further, in that having assumed full financial responsibility, the UN would then be free to dismiss any foreign staff and employ Ecuadorian doctors.'

Kara could not utter a word. She sipped her wine, her mind reeling under the duplicity and vindictiveness of her dead husband's family.

'Tell me,' Ross's deep voice broke into her thoughts, 'why does Beatriz hate you so much? It was obvious from what was said last night that she blames you for Luis's death. But there's something more, isn't there?'

Kara nodded slowly, staring into her glass. 'She and Luis were to have married. It had been accepted within the family since they were children. They may possibly have been engaged. I didn't even know Beatriz existed until I arrived in Quito after our marriage.'

'That explains quite a lot,' Ross murmured.

'What about?'

'Beatriz, your late husband and you,' Ross replied thoughtfully, and Kara looked away quickly from his piercing gaze. 'Why did he marry you? What had gone wrong between them?'

Kara put her head in her hands. 'I don't know. He refused to talk about her. He would simply withdraw, go completely silent if her name was mentioned.' She shrugged. 'Maybe she was mad with him for wasting his time on the Indians when he could have made a fortune in private practice. I don't know. As to his reasons for marrying me . . .' She glanced up at Ross. 'I often wonder,' she said softly. 'Looking back, we must have been a great disappointment to each other.' She caught herself and sat up, attempting a smile. 'And what was to be your reward for disposing of me?' She kept her voice light, though the pain was undeniable. 'How much money was my disappearance worth?'

Ross frowned in mock disgust. 'Nothing as sordid as money was mentioned.'

Kara looked blank. 'What then?'

Ross held her gaze. 'Beatriz made it abundantly clear that if I succeeded, what had been denied other, far more important and influential men, was mine for the asking.'

Kara suddenly understood and cursed her own naivety, 'You mean?'

'Exactly,' came the dry reply. 'In fact I was offered a discreet taste of the delights to come, but in the traditions of all those Sunday newspaper reporters, I made my excuses and left.'

'And that's not sordid?' Kara flared. She gulped her wine, then she rested her chin on one hand and her tone changed, becoming almost wistful. 'What confidence she must have. In her body, I mean—in her ability to please a man.'

'Don't you?' Ross lifted his glass, watching the flames through the pale liquid.

Kara opened her eyes wide. Her eyelids seemed determined to close. The warm fire and the hot food after the long trek had relaxed her. And the wine—the wine was delicious. It made everything easier. Talking was easier, and thoughts flowed like strands of honey, blending and separating, merging. 'Don't I what?'

'Have confidence in yourself as a woman?' The question was so gently put. His quiet voice, like rich, dark chocolate, neither challenging nor probing, sounded no alarms.

'Not much,' Kara admitted. 'I have a theory—' she hiccuped. 'Pardon me, I have a theory that it takes a man to give a woman real confidence in herself. Maybe it works the same in reverse too. But it's only a theory, untried, untested. Where were you born?'

'In Devon,' Ross took the abrupt change of subject in his stride.

'Have you got any family?' Kara drained her glass.

He nodded. 'My brother is an accountant in Plymouth and I've a married sister who lives in Germany. My parents settled in Devon when father retired from the army. I suppose I inherited my wander-lust from him. We were always on the move when I was a child. I can't remember how many schools I went to or how many countries I've lived in.' He grinned at the memory. 'What about you? Where does your family live?'

Kara turned the glass round and round on the table. 'My parents died in an accident when I was twelve. They left enough money to ensure I had a good education, and when I was home from boarding-school I used to stay with my Aunt Dorothy. A maiden lady devoted to her cats, her garden and good brandy.' She smiled up at Ross. 'After I qualified, I was offered, through friends of Daddy's, the chance of a twelve-month contract in Brazil. Aunt Dorothy pressed me to accept. She said it would broaden my horizons. She was finding the house a bit much to cope with and wanted to buy a little bungalow near the coast. I felt I'd been a burden to her for long enough, so we went our separate ways.'

'Was that where you met Luis? In Brazil?'

Kara nodded and her chin slipped off her hand. She replaced it, blinking thoughtfully. 'I was at a teaching hospital and Luis came to attend a seminar on the effects of vaccines on malnourished children.' Kara paused, looking back. 'He had so many plans,' she recalled softly. 'He was full of idealism. He wanted so much to change things, to improve conditions for the underprivileged people of his own country, but nothing seemed to happen fast enough for him. He used to get so impatient, but he didn't show it the way most people do, he kept it inside.'

Kara looked up at Ross. 'I don't think he knew how to cope when things went wrong. The family had always been his buffer against the world. I never saw him lose his temper, he would just turn in on himself. I couldn't reach him then, no one could. Sometimes it lasted for days.' There was a moment's silence.

'I never really knew him. Isn't that terrible? We were married for three years, yet I never knew him, not the way I feel I know—' some shred of sanity stopped her. She sat up slowly and pushed herself away from the table. 'I think—I think it's time I went to bed.'

What had happened to her? How many of her innermost thoughts had she let slip? It must have been the wine. She had no head for it and after the long day and the emergency with the children, two glasses had been quite enough to demolish her normal reticence.

Apprehension tightened her throat as she glanced uncertainly at Ross. He set his glass down on the table and, linking his hands behind his head, arched his body in a luxurious stretch. 'Sounds like a good idea,' he agreed. 'Almeida has insisted on doing the first four hours. I'll take over from her. The children will need more fluid and another dose of antibiotic.'

'But what about my turn?' Kara began.

'I'll call you when I get tired.'

She opened her mouth to protest, but Ross stood up, pushing his chair under the table. 'No arguments. Come on, just for once admit you're tired.'

Kara stifled a huge yawn. 'I am absolutely shattered.' She stood up as Ross poured hot water from the kettle into the pitcher.

'Go ahead,' he gestured, 'I'll bring this in for you.'

She collected the matchbox off the table and, weaving slightly, went through to her bedroom. With enormous concentration she managed to light her lamp and replace the glass, before a fit of giggles overcame her and she leaned against the wall as Ross poured water into the bowl. 'You know, I could get used to all this,' she sighed comfortably.

Ross straightened up, so close in the small room that she had to tilt her head back to see his face. He looked sombre as he traced the curve of her cheek with a forefinger, his dark eyes glittering in the soft light. 'So could I.' The words were almost inaudible. Then, turning away, he walked out, closing the door softly behind him.

The next four days were an oasis of peace and calm for Kara. Between them she and Ross unpacked and put away all the supplies and coped with the flow of patients to the clinic. During a few quiet moments Ross descaled the steriliser and Kara made up dressing packs. Almeida bustled about like a plump chicken with a large, unruly brood to fuss over, while Vicente worked slowly and steadily, planting further crops, cleaning out the animal pens, chopping wood and sharpening tools. And, to Kara's untold relief, the children began to respond mentally as well as physically to the treatment.

Even in the short time they had been receiving the vitamin-enriched milk and antibiotics, a definite improvement could be seen. Though they were still feverish, their skin was less dry and sallow and the rash was beginning to fade. Their eyes were not so blood-shot and sunken and their bodies, still painfully thin, had begun to flesh out. Their breathing was easier and the spasms of coughing less frequent.

But though the physical problems were lessening, others were beginning to reveal themselves. Strangely, it was the older boy who seemed most disturbed, refusing to drink the enriched milk even after Kara had tasted it herself to make sure it was palatable. Then he wouldn't do his breathing exercises.

'What is it? What's wrong?' Kara asked him gently, 'it doesn't still hurt when you breathe does it?'

The boy's glare was truculent, then he slowly turned

his head away. Two huge tears trembled on his lashes and spilled over to run down his cheeks. The grief and loneliness in his gesture tore at Kara's heart and suddenly she understood the reason for his behaviour.

'Listen,' she said softly, 'your mother didn't want to leave you. She was very brave to bring you here and it hurt her very much to go away. She'll be coming back for you as soon as you're better. We don't want to keep you here. We want you to get well as fast as you can so that you can go home with her.'

There was a long pause. Then, without turning his head, the boy sneaked a glance at her.

'I promise you she'll come back,' Kara repeated firmly, vowing she would cross the mountain herself to find the woman if she had to. 'Now, let's get you fit so that you'll be ready when she comes. Come on, now, drink your milk.'

With a sigh that caught on a sob, the boy did as he was told.

Ross was plainly delighted with the boys', recovery and had removed the drips on the third day. As they worked in the theatre, she preparing for outpatients while he made up the oral antibiotic the boys were having to replace the injection into the drip-tubing, he said over his shoulder, 'I haven't sailed that close to the wind for a long time. It really was touch and go for a while, especially with the younger child. Thank God their mother had the sense and courage to bring them here. Had she waited one more day, I don't think we'd have saved them.'

It gave Kara a shock to hear him identify himself so closely with the clinic and its patients. But the pleasure was mingled with pain as the question, never far from her mind, hung between them like a giant sword. How long would it take him to complete his assessment? How long before he announced he was leaving, moving on? How would she cope then with a sense of loss and loneliness far deeper than that she had known since Luis's death?

With a supreme effort of will she pushed those thoughts aside and concentrated on living moment by moment. It was almost uncanny how she and Ross, both used to working alone, made such a good team, each anticipating the other's needs, neither needing to assert authority, often not needing even to speak. Stranger still how the Indians had accepted it.

At mealtimes and in the evenings, whether they were still discussing medicine or had drifted on to other topics, there was an ease, an odd sort of trust between them, that could not be denied in spite of a surface wariness whenever the conversation became too personal. Then, on the evening of the fifth day, after a particularly demanding out-patient clinic, the idyll came to an abrupt end.

They were sitting at the dining table in the living room. Almeida had just brought in their meal of canned tuna fish, baked potatoes and salad, with dishes of fresh yoghurt and stewed apricots to follow. She was unloading the tray as Ross glanced across at Kara.

'I'm going down to Quito in the morning. It will mean you coping with the boys as well as outpatients and the ante-natal clinic, but it can't be helped.'

Kara's throat was dry, her heart thudded against her ribs. 'Is it important?' Her voice sounded strange and distant.

He nodded, picking up his knife and fork. 'Those damn drugs still haven't arrived and there's a limit to what we can treat with benzylpenicillin. My report to the UN is overdue, and there are one or two other matters that I must deal with.'

'Is better you not go,' Almeida interrupted, clutching the tray to her vast bosom, her chins wobbling in dismay.

Ross and Kara both looked at her in astonishment.

'You not go, Señor,' she wailed, 'is no good, I feel it

here.' Moving the tray she poked her chest, her finger almost disappearing into the heavily clothed mound.

'Almeida,' Kara began in a warning tone, but the other would not be silenced.

'Señora, all day I am uneasy, I sense something bad—'

'You'll sense something a lot worse if I don't get those drugs soon,' Ross said drily, beginning to eat.

Not sure whether Almeida's attack of clairvoyance was genuine or simply a ploy to try and keep Ross at the clinic, Kara had to fight against the despair that threatened to overwhelm her.

Ross must have read something in her expression, for with a touch of asperity he growled, 'Don't look like that, I'll be back in a couple of days.' At his words Almeida waddled out in a cloud of gloom.

Kara waited for Ross to say something more, something that would help her believe he really would come back, that he wasn't just trying to make the final parting easier by pretending it wasn't final, but he remained silent. Kara began slowly to eat, forcing the food down, holding her heart and her world together with sheer will power. 'Yes,' she said quietly, 'of course.'

CHAPTER SEVEN

SOMEBODY was there, Kara knew it. She could feel a presence. Close, coming closer. Her sleep had been disturbed, her dreams restless; broken images having no continuity, no meaning. Now underlying them she sensed something—someone—frightening—a threat . . .

With a cry, Kara jerked upright, then realised that the figure standing by her bed was Ross. 'What's the matter? What's wrong?' she blurted, her voice husky with sleep.

'Nothing's wrong,' he soothed. 'I didn't mean to startle you. I just looked in to say goodbye.'

'Oh.' Kara's heart, still bounding from the shock of her sudden awakening, plummetted.

'Don't look like that,' he growled, 'you don't know what it does to me.'

Drawing up her knees, Kara hugged them, throwing him a glance as she tossed her hair back over her shoulders. 'I expect you'll get over it,' she retorted, 'no doubt you've had plenty of practice.'

His face hardened. 'What's that supposed to mean?'

Kara studied her linked fingers rather than meet his gaze. 'Well, that's your style, isn't it? The pattern of your life, always moving, never staying long in one place. That's not a criticism,' she said quickly, 'it's a statement of fact.' She darted a look at him and wished she'd held her tongue. Anger and exasperation vied for precedence in his lean, tanned face.

'I've got to go, otherwise—' He sat down on the bed, seizing her shoulders, his strong fingers biting into her flesh. 'I don't know how long I'll be away. Maybe two days, maybe more. But I'm coming back,' he shook her, 'do you understand?'

'So you're coming back,' Kara's teeth chattered and she grabbed his arms, trying to loosen his grip. 'For how long this time?' The effort of suppressing her grief made her voice bitter and cynical.

'Damn you,' he muttered, and his arms enfolded her with a force that took her breath away. Her breasts were crushed against his chest and as he tangled his fingers in her hair and tugged, her head was forced back. His mouth ravaged hers with the anger and impatience of a conqueror.

Kara fought. Unable to free her arms, she hit his back as hard as she could with her fists. She tried to wrench her lips from his, but his strength was overpowering. Then suddenly she was falling. She hit the pillow with a thud, his full weight pressing her down onto the mattress. Hardly able to breathe, Kara began to panic. Her struggles became wilder, more erratic.

Ross tore his mouth from hers, but raised his face only a few inches. 'Just what is it with you?' he demanded hoarsely, studying her with an intensity that unnerved her.

Dragging air into her tortured lungs in great gasps, Kara stared back. 'What—what do you mean?'

'You're as prickly as a cactus,' he grated. 'One minute we're getting along fine, then without warning you've retreated into some secret stronghold and hoisted the drawbridge. What is it? Why do you keep me at such a distance?'

Shaken by the violence of his reaction, Kara pushed against his heavy shoulders. 'You could hardly be much closer,' she attempted to joke.

He grinned suddenly, a flash of white teeth in the gloom. 'Would you like to bet on that?' He moved his body on hers and Kara flushed deeply.

'No!' she cried. Oh God, what was she to do? How

could she tell him it was fear that made her act the way she did? She was afraid of so much. Afraid of being hurt again, afraid of loving him when he didn't love her, afraid that if he knew how she felt, the little time he remained would be clouded with discomfort and embarrassment. But her greatest fear was of her own reactions to him. While he held her like this she could feel his heart beating against her breast. Against her will the rhythmic pulse stirred an answering response in the deeper levels of her awareness.

The sensations she was experiencing were totally new to her. Her body, her arms and legs were growing warm and languorous. Instead of fighting him off she wanted to cling to him, to draw him closer, closer. Desire flickered, white hot, sending ripples of sensuality to tingle every nerve-ending.

Her body wanted him, her heart yearned for him, but her mind, still bearing the scars of the past, kept sounding the warning. If she loved, she would lose. If he came back after this trip, there would soon be another from which he would not return. It was his job, his life, just as she had said.

Why had it been him? Why couldn't the UN have sent somebody, anybody, else?

'Kara?' Ross murmured, running his lips over her cheek, her hair, her throat, an unmistakable urgency in his tightening clasp, his roughening voice.

'Look, I don't know what you want from me,' she cried desperately, now fighting both herself and him, 'but if it's just an affair, you'd be better off with Beatriz.'

Ross froze, then in one lithe movement, released her and stood up. His face was as bleak and cold as granite, his eyes glacial. 'You are one of the most infuriating women I have ever met,' the words squeezed out between gritted teeth. 'In fact, I can't think why I—' he shook his head impatiently. 'I'll be back as soon as I can.' His tone had changed completely, to become brisk and totally impersonal. 'Get as much sleep as possible, you'll need it.' He walked out without looking back, closing the door firmly behind him.

Kara tossed this way and that, unable to lie still, hating herself and him. Sharp claws of jealousy tore at her. What if he took her at her word? He was bound to see Beatriz while he was in Quito. He had probably intended to anyway, if only regarding the will and the family involvement. But even if he hadn't, no doubt Beatriz would seek him out.

Beatriz had made Ross an offer few men would refuse. After all, what did the clinic mean to him? It was only one job on a list of dozens as far as he was concerned. But he had turned her down. Yet she, Kara Noreno, doctor and prize fool, was virtually driving the man she loved into the waiting arms of a woman whose main aim in life was to destroy her. Brilliant move, Kara, she chided herself bitterly.

She flung back the blankets. She couldn't let him go like this, not with their parting words so angry and hostile. Maybe she could catch him before he left. But what would she say? She'd think of that when she reached him. Once she was with him the right words would come. She would apologise, try to explain . . .

Seizing her dressing-gown she stuffed her feet into her slippers, snatched open the door and raced through the sitting room to the kitchen, struggling to pull the robe around her as she ran, her hair tumbling wildly over her shoulders. Almeida was at the kitchen table, kneading bread dough with unusual violence, muttering beneath her breath. She looked up, startled, as Kara burst in.

'Has he gone yet?' Without waiting for an answer, Kara darted round the table.

'No, Señora, wait!' Almeida moved as if to stop her, but Kara already had the door open.

'Ross, Ross, I—' she stopped, as if hitting a wall, the words drying to dust in her mouth. It couldn't be. It wasn't possible. Her imagination was playing tricks on her.

Ross, holding No-name's bridle had his back to the door. '—don't want her to see you,' he was saying, 'you should not have come.'

'Good morning, Kara.' Beatriz ignored Ross, looking past him and down at Kara from the back of a well-groomed mule, her crimson mouth twisted into a spiteful smile. 'How cruelly harsh this early morning light can be. You look quite colourless.'

Automatically Kara pulled the robe more closely around her, horribly aware of being at a total disadvantage, neither washed nor dressed and her hair loose and tumbled, while Beatriz looked as though she had stepped off a magazine cover.

Her jacket and divided skirt were of soft black leather. Matching knee-length boots, polished to a mirror shine, rested in the stirrups. Beneath the jacket she wore a ruffled shirt of plum-coloured silk. Her hair was drawn tight and gleaming into a coil low on her neck, and her make-up, despite the early hour, was lavish and flawless. A flat-crowned sombrero hung down her back from a knotted leather cord. All this Kara took in in a split second.

Ross spun round. His face was thunderous and as his eyes met hers Kara shivered at their flint-like hardness.

'What, I mean—why?' she stammered, but before she could collect her thoughts sufficiently to frame the question, Ross was swinging himself up into the saddle. 'Get inside,' he ordered Kara harshly, 'you'll get chilled standing about out here.' He sawed savagely on the reins, causing No-name to rear and skitter sideways. He turned to Beatriz. 'You didn't come alone?'

She flashed him a dazzling smile. 'Of course not. Two of Francisco's vaqueros accompanied me. I left them to pack up, they will be waiting down the track. Come, Ross, we have a long way to go.' With a last contemptuous glance at Kara, Beatriz wheeled her mule around.

Digging her heels into the mule's side, Beatriz cantered off down the track. She rode superbly, moving as part of the powerful animal beneath her, the black sombrero bouncing against her back.

'Ross?' Bewildered and stricken, Kara involuntarily reached out a hand to him.

'Go back inside,' he repeated, his voice steel-edged. Their eyes locked and Kara saw something more in their depths. For an instant she thought he was going to say something, then Beatriz's voice floated back to them, imperious yet throaty, full of secret promise. 'Come, Ross.'

His jaw tightened and without a word he kicked the mule into a canter.

'Ross!' His name was an anguished whisper as Kara watched his broad back disappear over the bridge and down into the valley.

Almeida's hand on her arm brought Kara to her senses. 'Come, Señora, is much to do,' she said, her plump face doleful. 'You have coffee now?'

'Thank you.' The reply was automatic, but Kara felt she had to drag herself back from a far distant place. Everything seemed out of focus, disjointed. 'Did you know she was here, Almeida?' Kara sat down at the table.

Almeida did not meet her gaze, intent on pouring the coffee from the enamel jug into two mugs. 'No, Señora,' she said flatly, 'I not know till she knock on door and Señor Ross he open it.'

'You haven't seen her before?' Kara wasn't sure why she asked, but it seemed important. Was it possible that Beatriz had visited the village or the clinic when Luis was alive and she had not known about it?'

'No, Señora. She city woman,' Almeida was scornful, 'she no belong here.'

Then why had she come—to see Ross? Was it pure coincidence that brought her here just as he was leaving for the city? Why had he been so angry, why had he not explained? Just a word or two would have been enough. But he had denied her even that crumb of comfort.

Kara clasped her head in her hands, her mind reeling under the weight of questions to which she had no answers.

'Come, Señora, drink your coffee, the children they wake soon,' Almeida reminded her with a touch of impatience which was quite out of character.

Kara sat up and pulled the mug towards her, cupping it in her hands as if its warmth could drive out the chill in her heart. Almeida was right. She had a job to do. Ross would be back in a few days, then she would learn the reason for Beatriz's visit. Meanwhile, the only way to release the tension and cope with the restlessness was to work. This extra hour would give her a good start and she would ensure she kept far too busy to allow a single thought of either Ross Hallam or Beatriz Noreno to distract her.

But the day had already started under a cloud, thick and grey enough to match those outside. Nothing she did was able to fight off its dark shadow.

Almeida grew steadily more miserable. Not for her the tight-lipped, sullen pessimism of her Indian forebears. Her despair was as loud and dramatic as an Italian opera.

'Is not good he go,' she wailed. 'Why he no listen to me? His place here, with you, with us.'

'His place is wherever his job takes him,' Kara replied briskly, while her heart agreed with Almeida.

'Is trouble coming, I know it,' the older woman moaned, pushing the loaves into the oven.

Kara tried to ignore her, concentrating on mixing the children's liquid feed. But after the goat's milk had boiled over, two vitamin capsules squirted their contents into her face instead of into the bowl and she had knocked over the precious jar of vitamin C powder, even her determined equanimity had taken a severe knock.

Then, no doubt sensing the atmosphere, the children began to play up, refusing their feed, spitting out their medicine, knocking over the bowl as Kara tried to wash them, soaking sheets and blankets and leaving a puddle on the floor. Gritting her teeth, Kara held on to her temper. The expression on her face must have warned the boys that they'd gone far enough, for suddenly they changed, sitting quietly by the fire while Almeida changed the beds, taking the second lot of medicine without a murmur and doing their breathing exercises with great concentration.

Kara hid her smile, but beneath her amusement ran a thread of misery. Ross's absence was affecting everyone. It wasn't just her, even the children missed him. If it was like this now, after only a few hours, and he had promised to return, what on earth would it be like when he'd gone for good?

Stop. Don't think about it. One thing at a time. Just get through today, she warned herself. That promised more than enough problems if it continued the way it had started.

After rubbing the children's throats and chests with camphorated oil and liberally applying fresh calomine lotion to the few remaining spots, Kara grabbed a quick cup of coffee. Then it was time to open the doors of the clinic. The usual queue waited outside, but they were plainly uneasy. There were low murmurs and a restless shuffling of feet.

One after another they entered for dressings to be changed, medicines given and examinations made, but their eyes slid away from contact and their responses were guarded and monosyllabic. Getting information out of them was like drawing teeth, Kara thought crossly, as she completed a patient's card. How could she help if they wouldn't tell her what was wrong? Why did they come if they wouldn't trust her? Was Ross's absence affecting the villagers as well? Surely not. After all, he'd only been here just over a week. Was it that he was a better doctor than she? Or perhaps it was simply that tradition made the Indians more comfortable with a man.

In every aspect of her life it seemed events were conspiring to erode her confidence a fraction more each day. She went out to call the next patient, and there, at the back of the group, stood the brujo. He was watching her. Instead of the customary poncho, he was wearing an old jacket over his collarless shirt. While she noticed the change, it didn't occur to her to wonder where he'd got it from, for the brim of his felt hat dipped over eyes which, even at that distance, had the power to raise goose-pimples on her skin. He coughed, gargling the phlegm in his throat, and without shifting his gaze, spat with great deliberation into the dirt at his feet.

Tuberculosis was rife among the Andean Indians, and Kara was all too aware that the coughing and spitting practised by so many was one of the factors contributing to the spread of the disease. She and Luis had issued warning after warning. Whether the Indians refused to believe that their actions were responsible for the continuing toll of disease, or whether the habit was so ingrained they simply forgot, Kara wasn't sure. The brujo's action had been a deliberate insult and a challenge to her authority, but Kara knew this was no time for a showdown.

Forcing herself to turn casually away, to behave as though he were not there, Kara beckoned the old woman leaning against the wall. 'Will you come in now?'

The woman shuffled into the theatre and Kara followed her, her muscles tightening involuntarily as she turned her back on the brujo. Once the door was closed she gave herself a mental shake. She had to pull herself together. Life, and the clinic, had to go on with or without Ross Hallam.

So the morning passed. Outpatients took much longer than she expected. It was after one when the last patient left and she began clearing up. As she filled the steriliser it came home to her just how much of the routine work Ross had unobtrusively taken over.

She toyed with the idea of eating her lunch in the kitchen, but with Almeida being melancholy at full volume, Kara decided she couldn't face it. After a hasty bite, snatched while she completed some notes, she checked on the boys. Then, handing the washing to Almeida, she unlocked the theatre once more for the ante-natal clinic.

The first patient was six months into her third pregnancy. Though she had the typical squat roundness of the highland Indian, her weight owed more to her high carbohydrate intake then to her pregnancy.

It was useless to stress the necessity of a varied and well-balanced diet to people whose only source of food was what they could grow on the poor soil. Kara gave the woman a further supply of iron and vitamin tablets. Her general health was fairly good and though both she and the first child had had severe gastro-enteritis from which the baby had died, her second pregnancy and delivery had been straightforward and the little girl was only slightly underweight.

Kara made a mental note to broach the subject of birth control after this delivery. Three babies in under three years would tax the healthiest mother, but in these conditions the appearance of a fourth within twelve months was definitely not a good idea, for the whole family's sake.

The moment the second patient walked in, alarm bells began to ring in Kara's brain. As soon as the girl, for she was only eighteen, was on the table, Kara gave her a thorough examination. The rapid pulse, high blood pressure and swollen legs and feet indicated that the toxaemia Kara had suspected the previous week, was developing. When, in answer to Kara's questions, the girl admitted to headaches and dizziness with some nausea, the diagnosis was confirmed.

'I'd like you to stay here, in the ward next door,' Kara told the girl. 'Just until your baby is born, which should be in two weeks if all goes well.' She did not want to frighten the girl by warning her that unless the toxaemia was controlled the pregnancy would have to be terminated.

The girl promptly refused. 'I no stay. I go home.'

'It's only for a short time,' Kara assured her, 'you are not very well.'

'I all right. I go home.' The girl struggled to sit up.

'But why?' Kara helped her ease her legs over the side. 'You know me, you know the clinic. You are very near the village and all your family. I can look after you and your baby much better if—'

The girl shook her head, refusing to meet Kara's eye. 'I go home.'

'I can't force you, I wouldn't even try,' Kara said gently, 'but please, tell me why you won't stay.'

The girl pulled at her blouse, which gaped over her swollen belly, and Kara helped her fasten her skirt. 'The brujo,' she whispered, glancing around nervously, 'he tell my husband you go against the men, you steal babies from their parents and keep them hidden, and no one see what you do to them.'

Kara didn't know whether to laugh at such a ridiculous attempt at scare tactics or to scream with anger and frustration at the danger this girl and her baby were being subjected to. Controlling herself with great effort, she helped the girl off the table, folded the blanket around her shoulders and, taking her arm, led her to the inner door. 'I want to show you something.'

Both boys looked up, their eyes bright and alert. They

were threading hollowed-out chunks of bone of different shapes onto pieces of string. Vicente had made the crude toys, and they were absorbed in threading and unthreading the bones in different sequences.

'Say hello, boys,' Kara encouraged in Quechua. The soft croaks that issued from their swollen throats were barely recognisable, but there was no fear in either child's gaze, only mild curiosity.

'Are you ready for another drink?' she asked. Both boys nodded at once. The older one pointed at his mouth and made squeezing motions with his hands.

'You'd rather have fruit juice?'

They both nodded. Kara turned to the girl who was watching the children wide-eyed. 'Drinking lots of fresh fruit juice is part of the treatment to make them well again. Their mother carried them for two days over the mountain to bring them here so that we could help them. Would she have done that if she was afraid of us? Or if she thought we would harm her children?'

The girl edged towards the theatre and Kara knew it was useless to press further. Regardless of what she had seen with her own eyes, the influence of her husband, her father and the brujo was too strong.

'I'll be back in a moment, boys,' Kara called over her shoulder as she walked with the girl to the outside door. 'You must rest as much as you can,' she warned. 'That means lying down, not working in the house or the fields.'

Kara debated for a moment whether to give the girl a diuretic, or sedatives in an effort to lower her blood pressure, but decided against it. Unless the girl was in the ward where her pulse, blood pressure and fluid intake and output could be closely monitored, the risks attached to the medication were greater than not giving any.

'Shall I come and see you tomorrow?' Kara suggested. 'Then you won't have to walk up to the clinic.' The girl looked worried and shook her head. Knowing any added stress would only make matters worse, Kara didn't argue. 'Will you rest all day tomorrow, then come and see me the next day?'

The girl hesitated, then with a muttered, 'Yes,' she lumbered out of the clinic and moved slowly down the path. Another, older woman was waiting for her by the bridge. Her mother maybe? Kara watched them cross the stream in an agony of frustration.

Would Ross have been able to persuade her to stay? The Indians had responded so quickly to him. Since Luis's death she had had a constant battle against the in-built resistance of the men to taking orders from a woman. She understood and accepted that many of them tolerated rather than welcomed her, and then merely because she offered the only alternative when the brujo's mixture of witchcraft and folk-medicine failed. The fact that Ross was a male doctor weighed more heavily with the Indians than their automatic mistrust of strangers. That was progress of a kind, even if it did relegate her to the lowest rank. But provided disease was controlled and suffering eased, what did status matter?

As she went back inside she closed the door with a firmness that gave some indication of the pressure within her and went to slice oranges for the boys, relieved that Almeida was out in the wash-house. When they were once more settled, she opened the door for the mother and baby clinic, wondering with unusual pessimism how many would bother to come. Almost to her surprise, four turned up. There was a marked reticence among them, an anxiety to get the examination over and leave quickly, but Kara attributed that to the work still to be done on potato planting.

As she weighed the babies, examined ears and throats, listened to hearts and lungs, flexed and extended tiny limbs and administered vaccinations, Kara tried to shake off her depression. She had allowed Almeida's premonitions to overshadow her own common sense. As far as the clinic was concerned, financial problems apart, things looked good. There was still a long way to go, but the mothers were coming reasonably regularly now to have their babies' progress monitored. It showed she was gaining their confidence, and preventive care was equally as important as treatment.

At last, after the boys had been fed and washed and the routine checks made, Kara decided to call it a day. It was almost seven. She sat down in front of the single place set on the dining table and, putting her elbows on the dark wood, rested her head in her hands.

Almeida shuffled in with her evening meal. 'I sit with the boys while you eat?' she asked dully.

Kara gave her a weary smile. 'That would be a help. I think tomorrow I'll let them get up for a while. They'll enjoy the change and they'll realise they really are moving towards going home.'

'Si, Señora,' Almeida muttered tonelessly, and waddled out.

Kara stared after her, then shrugged helplessly and turned her attention to the food. As she ate, the silence crowded in on her. Ross filled her mind. How she missed him. Mealtimes had developed into an occasion to talk over the day's work, to discuss and often argue over preferred techniques of treatment, his wider experience in combat with her knowledge of local people and conditions. Then, with the coffee, the conversation usually drifted to other topics, books, music, places, ideas, as they bounced opinions off one another, surprised and yet not surprised when their tastes coincided.

How vivid was the contrast with her meals with Luis, the obligatory reading and the long silences, fraught with tension. She looked across at the empty chair where Luis had once sat, where now she was used to seeing Ross, longed to see Ross.

How angry she had been that first couple of days. Ross had been an intruder, an outsider destroying with brutal unconcern the memories she had tried so desperately to preserve. Now, with the startling clarity he had brought into her life she saw that those pictures of the past were only a myth. They had no substance. They had been a distortion of the truth, her protection against reality.

Was that what Ross had meant in the hotel, when he had told her that sooner or later she would have to face reality? She had thought afterwards he was referring to the family, but his words applied equally to this.

As she looked back on her marriage, Kara realised that her mourning was over, that her grief had been not for what she had lost, but for what she had never known. Clearly and calmly she faced the fact that, in all personal aspects, her marriage to Luis had been a failure. Both had married for the wrong reasons. She to share an ideal, to belong to a family and to have someone of her own, and Luis—who knew what his real reasons were?

Yet for all the anguish, guilt and self-recrimination the brief marriage had caused her, she could not regret that it had happened. It had brought her to a job she loved in a country that fascinated her. And she had grown up. She had learned much about people generally and herself in particular. But it had been a gradual process, and the full realisation of what she had learned had only dawned since the arrival of Ross Hallam.

He had awakened emotions in her heart and sensations in her body she had not dreamed existed. There was no future with him and quite how she was going to cope, she had no idea. But one thing she was sure of, the past was dead and had to be left where it belonged.

Kara stretched out her left hand, studying for a moment her long fingers with their short, oval nails. Then, deliberately, without effort, she drew off the slim, gold wedding ring. She paused, holding it between thumb and forefinger, thinking of all the hopes and dreams it had signified, then she stood up and slipped it into the hip pocket of her cords. It had no significance now, it was simply an item of jewellery. The next time she went into the capital, she would sell it. Any extra money would be useful for the clinic.

Almeida crept out of the ward. 'They ready to sleep,' she whispered.

'I'll look in and say good-night, then I'll be in theatre for a while. I've still got some tidying up to do and I want to make up some fresh dressing packs. Will you ask Vicente to start the generator? I'll use the lights instead of oil-lamps.'

Almeida nodded and went out. Her voluble warnings of disaster had been replaced by a grim silence. While it was a relief on one hand, so pervasive was her attitude of impending doom, that Kara felt herself growing uneasy. Trying to dismiss the disquiet she resolved to bury it in her usual antidote to problems, both personal and professional—work.

She had been in the theatre about an hour and a half when Almeida rushed in, nervous and excited, making Kara jump. 'Señora, in the village, something is happening.' Her voice was a raucous whisper. She had remembered, despite her agitation, the sleeping children. 'There is much noise, shouting, I don't know what. You come quick.' She scurried out again. Kara dropped the dressings she was packing into the sterilizer drum and ran after her.

Standing together just outside the kitchen door they could hear the shouts. Kara frowned as she realised the noise was coming nearer. She listened intently, then it dawned. 'They're drunk,' she murmured, then turned to Almeida, completely puzzled. 'But chicha beer usually just sends them to sleep, when they can get enough of it. I've never known them react like this.' Almeida shrugged and pulled a face, then Kara's voice took on a new urgency. 'Quick, where's Vicente?'

'He brush the mules, I think.'

'Tell him to let out all the animals and scatter them.'

Almeida was shocked, 'But Señora, how we find them again?'

'Let's worry about that tomorrow,' Kara said briskly. 'Right now I'm more concerned with what might happen to them at the hands of a drunken mob. I'll turn off the generator and start closing the shutters. You make sure all the outhouses are locked.'

'You think is danger?'

'I don't know what to think, but something has stirred those men up and they aren't coming this way for a social chat, so hurry.'

Almeida waddled away as fast as her short legs would carry her. Kara ran to shut down the generator. As the motor died and the lights went out in the operating-theatre, the uproar was suddenly much louder. Rough and slurred the voices bawled. Then she heard the crash and tinkle of breaking glass.

Her hands froze on the lock. Glass? The Indian houses had no windows and chicha was brewed in clay or earthenware pots. Chills danced down her spine. The men were smashing bottles.

As Kara sprinted across to the clinic and began slamming the shutters, snapping the padlocks closed with fingers that had become thumbs, her mind was racing. This was a poor village, they could barely support themselves. They could not possibly afford to buy alcohol.

Vicente appeared beside her. 'You go inside, Señora, I do this,' his gravelly voice urged.

'The animals, are they—'

'All gone, over hillside. Now you go quick.'

Kara ran down to the kitchen door as Almeida puffed across from the wash-house with two buckets of water.

'Maybe we no can get more tonight,' she gasped. Kara took one from her and they dropped them inside the door, then rushed back to look down the path.

The mob had reached the bridge. Kara could hardly believe what she was seeing. The normally sullen, impassive Indians had been transformed into a staggering, howling rabble. Three of them waved crude torches made from flaming branches that cast a flickering orange glow across frenzied faces.

'Lord have mercy on us,' Almeida muttered, crossing herself rapidly.

'The roofs,' Kara cried, 'if they burn the thatch—how much water have we got?' She spun round scanning the kitchen.

'Two buckets, the pitcher and the kettle, Señora,' Almeida answered promptly, 'not enough.'

'All shutters locked, Señora,' Vicente appeared in the doorway. He had to raise his voice to be heard above the rising clamour outside.

'The Señora, she think they set fire to roofs,' Almeida babbled in a flurry of waving arms.

'Is no time to wet them,' he growled, 'must put out torches.' He seized one of the buckets and raced across the path at a crouching run to hide between the washhouse and the feed store, just as a stone thudded into the dirt a few inches from Kara, who flinched. It was the signal for a hail of missiles. One hit Kara's shoulder, knocking her sideways. They thumped onto the thatched roof and crashed against the stone walls. She stared uncomprehendingly at the mark on her sweater. This couldn't be happening. It must be a nightmare and she'd wake up in a minute. Then another stone bit into her thigh, and Almeida yanked her backwards into the safety of the kitchen.

'I don't understand,' Kara murmured blankly, 'it doesn't make sense. Why are they doing this?'

'Señora, quick, bring bucket,' Almeida was peeping

through a crack in the door. 'It no matter why, only matter how long. We find out why another day.'

'You've certainly changed since this morning,' Kara observed, as she put the bucket down by Almeida's feet.

Almeida took her eye from the crack for a moment and Kara was amazed to see her plump face crease in a grin. 'Si. It happen like I say. Two days I warn, I beg Señor Ross not to go.'

'You didn't know this was going to happen?' Kara began horrified.

'Not this, something. I—'

'Almeida, if you say "I told you so"—' Kara warned, but Almeida interrupted her.

'They close now. Vicente he will take two at front. I open door quick and you throw water over one in middle.'

Kara felt her stomach knot. Apprehension mixed with a dreadful excitement as adrenalin poured into her veins, charging her with nervous energy, sharpening her reflexes, poising her for action. She gripped the handle of the bucket tightly, her other hand holding the base. A stone crashed against the door, then another. The din was indescribable.

'Ready, Señora,' Almeida shouted, 'now!' She pulled open the door, Kara darted forward into the opening and hurled the water with all her strength.

The flames were dowsed and the torch bearer gasped and coughed, then roared with rage at the unexpected drenching. Vicente had also been successful and was laying about him with the bucket as the men, suddenly blind, cannoned into each other, roaring obscenities and reeling under the influence of alcohol.

Almeida was shrieking at the top of her voice through the gap in the door, as Vicente fought to reach the safety of the clinic. Then, from behind her, Kara heard a wail.

The children! In the panic, Kara had forgotten them. They were quite safe, but the noise would terrify them. Kara couldn't leave the door, Almeida would never hold it on her own. Vicente, having abandoned the bucket, was still struggling with one stocky Indian who was trying to hit him with a bottle.

Vicente lashed out at the man and managed to free himself, but as he spun away, the Indian's flailing arm, still clutching the bottle by the neck, crashed against Vicente's skull. The glass smashed, the shards tinkling onto the ground.

Kara held her breath as Vicente, grunting with pain and exertion, dived for the door and fell into the kitchen.

Kara and Almeida slammed it shut, and shot the bolts home, ignoring the howls as the Indians' bare feet were lacerated by the fragments of broken glass.

'Go and comfort the children,' Kara ordered Almeida who was staring at the prostrate body of her husband. 'And turn up all the lamps, let's have some light in this place.' She could hear the tremor in her voice and swallowed hard. 'Go on, Almeida, they need you. I'll see to Vicente. I don't think he's badly hurt.' As she bent down and turned his head from side to side, Vicente groaned and opened his eyes.

'He got thick skull, that man,' Almeida grinned, her eyes glistening, and she turned away quickly as her mouth quivered. 'All right, my little heroes,' she sang, as she bustled away to the ward. 'I am coming, is nothing to fear, nothing to worry.'

With the doors closed and the shutters over the windows, the noise was less frightening. But there was no way of seeing what was happening outside.

Kara poured hot water from the kettle into a jug and, instructing Vicente to remain exactly where he was, she went through to the theatre. Almeida was crooning to the boys who lay wide-eyed against the white pillows, flinching each time a stone rattled against the shutters

She smiled reassuringly at the boys, lit the lamps with fingers that still trembled slightly and quickly prepared a dressing tray. Then, grabbing a wad of gauze, she hurried back to the kitchen.

Vicente had struggled to his feet and was swaying as he clutched at the table.

'Come on, let's get that cut seen to.' Kara put her arm around his waist and tugged his other arm over her shoulder. He resisted.

'No, Señora,' he mumbled, 'I servant, no touch.'

Kara could have screamed. Letting go with one arm she thrust the gauze into his hand. 'Hold that against your head, but don't press. I don't want the children to be frightened by the blood. Now come on.' She half-dragged, half-supported him out of the kitchen, but as they reached the ward door, Vicente, dredging up some hidden reserves, straightened. 'I walk alone, Señora. No frighten children.'

With a sigh, Kara released him. He staggered slightly, then with slow deliberation he shuffled through the ward. As soon as they caught sight of the blood-stained gauze, both children pointed and the hoarse croaks which issued from their throats were obviously demands to know what had happened.

'Vicente was slightly injured but he'll be fine,' Kara said briskly, edging him forward. Another flood of questions tumbled out. Kara would have ignored them but Vicente, with a grin that was more a grimace of pain, murmured to the boys in Quechua, sending them into peals of laughter.

'What did you say?' Kara demanded suspiciously.

'Señora, I tell them the truth, that a man hit me on the head with a bottle, but my head is so tough, I break the bottle, then I hit him plenty times and he now feeling much worse than me.'

Kara shook her head. What could she say? Far from frightening the boys, they obviously thought it great fun.

No doubt they would beg Vicente to tell them the story over and over again.

As she cleaned and stitched the ugly gash, her mind, soothed by the familiar activity, shook off the blanket of shock and bewilderment, and she began to think coherently.

Why had the Indians gone on the rampage? Surely the brujo alone couldn't have incited them to such an action? Was it over the children? Kara dismissed the idea. That simply wasn't sufficient reason.

Where had the alcohol come from? The smell of the cheap spirit was sharp in her nostrils where it had splattered over Vicente's hair and clothes in the struggle. To have supplied them with enough to rouse them to this pitch would have cost quite a lot of money. Who around here had any money, anyway? Round and round the questions went until Kara thought her head would burst.

The irregular thud of stones hitting the shutters was lessening, and the raucous shouting faded as the rabble moved away from the buildings. What would they do now? Kara could only pray that the depressive effect of the alcohol would soon overcome their frantic activity and plunge them into drowsiness and stupor.

But why, and who? Kara taped a wad of gauze over the sutured wound to protect it. 'Go straight to bed, Vicente. It's possible you might have a mild concussion, and in any case there's nothing more any of us can do tonight.'

'Si, Señora,' he swung his legs off the table and made for the door.

'And no more action replays for the children tonight,' she called after him, 'you need sleep and so do they.'

'Si, Señora,' the bland reply floated after him as he closed the door, leaving Kara in theatre to begin clearing up.

As she washed the instruments in antiseptic and put

them aside for sterilising the following day, Kara's thoughts turned once again to fret at the questions, who and why?

She turned out the lamps, picked up the bucket containing the soiled gauze and cotton wool, the jug and the bowl and left the theatre, locking the door behind her. The boys grinned drowsily as she passed them. Almeida had obviously allayed all their fears—or, more likely, Vicente had promised them a blow-by-blow account in the morning if they went to sleep now.

Throwing the rubbish on the fire, Kara emptied the bowl into a slop bucket. Almeida peered out from her curtained alcove. 'You want I make you some coffee, Señora?' she whispered.

Kara shook her head. 'You get some sleep. God knows what we'll find outside in the morning.' She poured hot water into the pitcher and went through to her bedroom. She had a good wash, slipped on her nightdress and a dressing-gown and brushed her hair until it crackled. Still she could not relax. She went to the window and listened intently. All the noise had ceased. The only sound was the muted hiss of a sudden heavy shower.

At least that would put paid to any ideas of firing the thatch, Kara thought thankfully. Hopefully it would also drive any of the men still conscious back to their homes.

She looked at the bed and knew she would not sleep. She crept into the sitting room and sat on the settee, drawing her legs up beside her. The fire had been out for some time and grey ash filled the grate, but Kara wasn't cold.

Who and why?

It was a scheme almost diabolical enough for the family to have devised, she thought fleetingly, then stiffened. Would they really go to such lengths? She knew the answer even as the question formed. But why? Until Ross's arrival they were winning anyway. Even if they were involved they would have to have an ally here. The brujo? Assuming they would deal with an Indian at all, would they be able to rely on him doing what they wanted? And what about the liquor? No Indian would have been able to purchase that amount of alcohol without causing a lot of interest and suspicion. Besides, someone would have had to give him the money in advance, that was the way the witch-doctors worked. They got paid first and if their cure didn't work then it was not their fault but due to some wrong-doing by the patient, or even the anger of the gods.

No, there had to be someone else involved.

A brief, clear memory of Beatriz, her smile malicious and taunting, flashed through Kara's mind. Had Beatriz known what was to happen? Could she have had some part in it? Surely not, for if Ross had been present Kara was quite sure he would have been able to defuse the situation before the mob had gone on the rampage. Besides, Beatriz could not possibly have known that Ross was leaving the clinic to go to the capital, leaving Kara alone, with only Vicente and Almeida for company and protection—he had only decided to go the evening before.

How do you know? a small insistent voice within her argued. He only told you that evening, he might have planned it days ago, at the dinner party after you left.

Kara shook her head, trying to banish the treacherous doubts. Ross had been furious, and she had heard him tell Beatriz she shouldn't have come.

Kara shivered, recalling his bleak expression as he turned and saw her, and his voice, cold and commanding, ordering her back into the house. The same man who, only minutes before, had held her in his arms, crushing her, still warm from sleep, beneath his weight, kissing her with passionate urgency. The same voice that had murmured her name like a caress as desire mounted in both of them.

Which was the real Ross? And who had provoked his terrible anger, Beatriz or herself?

If it was Beatriz, why had he ridden away with her, without so much as a backward glance, without a word of explanation? And if it was herself he was furious with, why? Kara could not help thinking that if she had remained in bed a few minutes longer, if she had resisted the impulse to speak to him just once more before he left, she would not have seen Beatriz, would have known nothing of her visit. Unless Ross had told her on his return. What did it matter? Unless he had something to hide. Unless he was in some way involved with Beatriz.

Kara's hand, resting on the leather arm of the settee, clenched suddenly as a shaft of unspeakable pain lanced through her. Oh God, it couldn't be that, not him. Not Ross.

CHAPTER EIGHT

THE MOUNTAINS cast dark shadows as the rising sun crept over the peaks. There was no warmth in the golden rays, but it was not only the early morning chill that made Kara shiver as she thrust her hands deep into the pockets of her old anorak.

She forced her gaze back to the vegetable plots. Tears filled her eyes and she shook her head, angrily blinking them away as she kicked jagged stones off the path. Beside her Vicente smouldered, tight-lipped and furious, the white dressing on his temple in stark contrast to his brown, weathered skin.

Kara swallowed hard. So much effort, so quickly and senselessly destroyed. 'You'd better get the animals back first, Vicente, then we'll decide what to do about all this.' She gestured helplessly towards the trampled earth, strewn with torn-up broken plants, and turned back to the house.

She walked down the path, kicking aside the chunks of rock that had been thrown at the clinic the previous night. As she bent down to pick up some needle-sharp shards of glass glistening in the dirt, she noticed movement out of the corner of her eye. An Indian woman was coming over the bridge.

Instinct told Kara to run, to get into the house. Then common sense took over. The woman was alone, and she was in a hurry. As she drew nearer, moving with the short-stepped trot peculiar to South American Indians, Kara recognised her as the woman waiting by the bridge the previous afternoon, and knew there could be only one reason why she had come. Something must be wrong.

Kara gave no greeting. Holding the broken glass, she stood up and waited for the woman to reach her.

'My daughter, something wrong,' the woman paused.

'Has her labour started?' Kara asked expressionlessly.

'No, no, is a devil in her,' the woman quickly mimed the successive facial twitching, rigidity and jerking movements of a convulsion, and with dread Kara realised the girl's toxaemia had developed into eclampsia. 'You come now,' the woman demanded.

'Why don't you ask the brujo?' Kara retorted bitterly, the devastated garden still fresh in her mind.

'He drunk, he can do nothing,' the woman's impatience was plain. 'You come.'

Kara began to laugh, shaking her head. They had wrecked her garden, stoned the clinic, and injured Vicente. Her own shoulder and thigh were bruised where missiles had struck them and yet she was expected to forget that and devote all her experience to saving the life of a girl who had refused the treatment which could have prevented her present condition. To cap it all the woman had admitted she had gone to the brujo first and that she, the doctor, was second choice.

Why should I? Kara stared at the glass in her hands, her laughter fading as rage, misery and utter desolation washed over her in a tidal wave. Why the hell should I? I don't owe them a thing.

The woman shuffled her calloused, bare feet in the dirt. 'You come now,' she demanded.

Kara looked at her, saw the dirty clothes, the traditional designs almost obscured, saw the rough, weather-beaten skin of hands, feet and face, the cracked, broken nails and stooped posture that told of a lifetime's hard labour. And she saw the worry in the woman's black eyes.

'Wait here,' she said abruptly, 'I'll get my bag.' Of course she would go. It was her job. It was the reason she was here. What happened last night was not the girl's fault. For all those who did not trust her there were others who did, and for those who wished her to leave there were others who needed her to stay. Besides, she did owe them, she owed them her knowledge, her ability to help them help themselves. Gratitude was not part of the bargain and she had no right to expect it.

She dumped the glass in a bucket to be disposed of later, washed her hands quickly and started collecting the things she needed. As she packed the sphyg, thermometer and her stethoscope, Kara's brain switched over to the medical problems she was likely to encounter. The girl would need an immediate sedative. Something by mouth would have been ideal but it would take too long to act. She would have to inject diazepam, despite the risk of venous thrombosis. Swiftly preparing the syringe and wrapping it in a sterile towel in a dish, Kara snapped her bag shut and ran out of the theatre, calling to Almeida as she went. 'I'll check the children when I get back, just wash and change them for now. But first find Vicente and send him after me with the stretcher.'

'Si, Señora, you want I cook lunch and clean house as well before I go?' Almeida demanded tartly, up to her elbows in washing-up.

As Kara followed the woman into the village, she saw several men sleeping where they had fallen. One still clutched an empty bottle. Their feet were caked and streaked with blood and their clothes were sodden from the rain and spattered with mud. Her gaze swept over them and she walked on.

Passing several houses she felt eyes on her, and once she glanced around just in time to see a head swiftly withdrawn from a doorway. She trod down her nervousness. She had seen all of these people in the clinic at one time or another. Her heart thumped faster, her mouth was dry. There was nothing to be frightened of. She was not here uninvited, seeking revenge, her presence had been sought, demanded. Her stride faltered. What if it was a trap? She swallowed hard. If it was, it was too late to back out now, she was right in the middle of it.

Several women stood outside one of the stone hovels. The girl's mother pushed through them, lifted a blanket hanging over the doorway and beckoned Kara in. Ducking her head, Kara followed, and saw, lying on a dirty blanket on the bare earth floor, the girl jerking in the grip of a convulsion. Immediately, Kara forgot everything else.

'Take that blanket down and ask those people to get back from the doorway,' Kara ordered the mother. 'I must have light to see what I'm doing, and your daughter needs some fresh air.' The foetid smell of unwashed bodies and stale cooking was thick in the small house. Crouching beside the girl, Kara opened her bag.

Several minutes later she heard Vicente's voice. Leaning out of the doorway, she waved to him. As soon as he reached her she explained, 'We must get this girl to the clinic fast. I'll need you to help me get her onto the stretcher, but we must be as gentle as possible. Although she's under sedation, any sudden noise or movement could trigger another convulsion.' Kara knew she was taking a terrible risk in moving the girl at all, but trying to treat her where she was would be condemning both her and her baby to certain death.

With Vicente in front, the girl's husband carried the rear end of the stretcher. His skin was a sickly colour, his eyes bloodshot, and his hands trembled. Kara wondered what was wrong with him until she smelled the alcohol on his clothes and his breath. From the expression on his face, Kara guessed he was suffering, and she hoped fiercely it was a hangover he would never forget.

With the girl's mother at one side, Kara at the other and the women tagging along behind, the little procession wound its way up to the clinic. Kara unlocked the outside door to the theatre and they eased the unconscious girl carefully onto the operating-table. 'Start the generator, please. I'll use the lights,' Kara directed Vicente.

'The shutters, Señora?' Vicente began

'Leave them closed. If they look in,' Kara indicated the women hanging about outside, 'and don't like what they see, or if the brujo wakes up and decides to complain about breach of ethics by putting a few rocks through the window, this girl's chances will be zero.'

As Vicente left, the girl's mother and her husband turned to leave, anxious to get away from surroundings which clearly made them uneasy.

'One of you has to stay,' Kara stated quietly. Husband and mother stared, blank-faced at her, then at each other. The young man shook his head, winced, then jerking his thumb at his mother-in-law, stumbled unsteadily outside. The woman shrugged.

'As soon as she's stable, I will have to induce labour, bring the baby early,' Kara explained. 'Have you attended childbirth before?' The woman nodded. 'Then until I'm ready, you just sit there and don't move.' Kara pointed to the stool by the bench, knowing she sounded curt and totally unlike herself, but past caring.

'Why you want I stay?' the mother demanded suspiciously.

'Partly because I'll need your help later, and partly because whatever happens in the next twelve hours, you are going to witness that I do everything in my power to save the lives of both your daughter and her baby. Though, thanks to ill-informed gossip which frightened your daughter out of coming here when she should have, the odds are against it.' The mother sat down and Kara began to work.

First she checked the girl's temperature, pulse rate, respiration and blood pressure, and entered them on a fresh chart, noting the time. Those readings would be repeated at close, regular intervals. Next, after gently swabbing the girl's legs and abdomen, she inserted a catheter to drain the bladder, relieving internal pressure on the uterus. Then, after carefully turning the girl onto her side, supporting her with pillows, Kara hauled the cylinder of pure oxygen and that of oxygen and nitrous oxide to the head of the operating-table. The first was in case of further convulsions, the second for possible use once labour was under way. Next Kara prepared an injection of magnesium sulphate. This would act as an anti-convulsant and help to reduce the girl's temperature.

Immersed in her task, Kara gradually forgot the girl's mother, perched on the stool like a squat black crow. She forgot everything but the two lives that depended entirely upon her. When Almeida put her head around the door two hours later, Kara was startled at how quickly the time had flown.

'Señora, you want coffee?' she whispered.

Kara unhooked her stethoscope and gestured for Almeida to wait while she entered the latest readings on the chart. Stripping off her gown, she went quietly across to the door. 'Can you sit in for me while I examine the boys and give them their medicine?'

Almeida looked doubtful, but Kara reassured her. 'The convulsions are under control now and she's resting.'

'People coming up from the village,' Almeida whispered. 'More women, but some men too. Some not walk good.'

'What do you mean? Are they injured?' Kara remembered the crashing bottles, the glass on the path and the howls of pain.

'Some, yes. But others, they hide eyes from sun, their faces the colour of mutton fat and they sway—' Almeida rolled her eyes and lurched alarmingly.

Kara's eyebrows lifted. 'With hangovers like that, what are they doing up here?'

Almeida shrugged. 'I not know, Señora, they just wait.'

'They surely don't expect me to treat them?'

Almeida shrugged again.

'Well, if they do, they're going to be disappointed.' She washed her hands, then collected the bottle of antibiotic, two spoons, her stethoscope, thermometer and auriscope. 'Let them suffer,' she muttered to herself, 'and while they're suffering, I hope they remember who was responsible.' Then leaving Almeida standing with arms folded, wearing responsibility like a banner, Kara went out of the theatre into the ward.

As she carefully examined each boy, noting with pleasure the continuing improvement in their general condition, she told them they would be able to sit by the fire in the kitchen for a while later in the afternoon and watch Almeida cook. Their eyes shone with excitement at the prospect of leaving their beds, and they could hardly keep still for Kara to finish listening to their chests. Then, giving them each a drink of hot lemon and honey and a sheet of paper and a pencil, she swallowed her cold coffee and returned to the theatre.

She told Almeida about the plan to move the boys into the kitchen. 'It's not simply to relieve their boredoom. I don't know how things will go in here, and if there's an emergency or a lot of noise I don't want them frightened.' Last night had been bad enough.

As she slipped her arms into the gown, turning for Almeida to do up the tapes, she felt a moment's dizziness as once more, like an avalanche, a sense of betrayal almost suffocated her. Was it you, Ross? Did you leave, knowing what was going to happen? It was almost unbearable. The anguish in her heart made her feel physically ill, such was its intensity, and for several seconds she had to fight to regain her mental balance.

At one-thirty Kara checked the girl's vital signs yet again. The pulse rate was starting to climb, so was the blood pressure. Kara dared wait no longer. The baby's heart rate was up, a sure sign of foetal distress. She had no choice but to induce labour at once, and hope to save one of them. With a new urgency in her swift silent movements, Kara set up the IV apparatus and began the slow infusion of oxytocin that would stimulate the girl's womb to start contracting.

The next six hours ticked by like the slow fuse on a time bomb. Kara was on a tightrope. Oxytocin was known to produce side-effects of high blood pressure and violent contractions which might trigger new convulsions.

The girl's groans rose to a shout as each pain gripped her. With infinite care Kara injected a combination of pethidine and promethozine in an effort to dull the pain and calm the patient, who was writhing and gasping.

Kara was also intensely concerned for the baby, whose heartbeat was now irregular. Whether this was due to the oxytocin or to the effects of the earlier convulsions, she had no way of knowing.

Kara decided to examine the girl once more to see how far the dilation had progressed. But just as she was snapping on fresh gloves, the girl began to grunt and strain, curling her body round as she pushed.

Kara called to the girl's mother who stood uncertain, overawed by all that was happening. 'Hold her hand, talk to her. Come on, you've done this before, forget where you are. She's having your grandchild, tell her how well she'd doing,' Kara urged, and the woman began, nervously at first, then with growing confidence to encourage the girl.

As the tiny head emerged, Kara swabbed its eyes. The little face was blue, and Kara knew the next few minutes were crucial. 'Come on, you're doing fine,' she coaxed, trying to keep the anxiety out of her voice, 'your baby is almost here. One more push.'

The girl's body tautened, then with a rush the rest of the tiny body appeared. The girl collapsed exhausted and panting as Kara turned the baby upside down to clear its air passage. It hung limp from her hands, and Kara's heart stood still as she gave the little bottom a sharp slap.

'Breathe,' she muttered, 'breathe.' She slapped again, and the baby's chest fluttered as a thin wail of protest issued from its blue lips. The wail became a howl and Kara laid the baby down to clamp and cut the cord, then wrapped it in a clean towel, rejoicing in the lusty roar that was expanding the tiny lungs and sending life-giving oxygen to turn its skin dusky pink.

Kara held the baby close for a moment, then lay him in the crook of his mother's arm. 'You have a son.'

The girl looked up at Kara. Her haggard face, with dark circles beneath drug-dulled eyes, was transformed by a soft smile, so radiant it brought a lump to Kara's throat. 'My son,' she whispered.

Kara knew the danger was not over yet. The girl would need to be watched carefully over the next week, but the greatest hurdle was behind them. And she'd done it. Her first case of eclampsia, and she'd brought bought mother and baby through alive! Just wait till she told Ross. Then she remembered and bent her head as agony engulfed her. It couldn't be true, he couldn't have known. Yet she had heard him say he didn't want her to see Beatriz. Could they have planned something together? Could they be in league? But he had cared. He had worked alongside her. He had involved himself with every aspect of the clinic . . . She realised the girl's mother was speaking to her.

'What? What did you say?'

The woman lifted the baby gently from her daughter's arms and repeated, 'I show them.'

'Who?' Kara struggled to concentrate on what the woman was saying as she dealt with the afterbirth.

'They wait outside, I show them baby.'

'Just a minute.' Kara opened the ward door and shouted, 'Almeida!' The rotund figure of her housekeeper appeared in seconds, anxiety pinching her face. 'It's a boy,' Kara told her, and Almeida's face exploded in a smile. 'Can you open the shutters from the outside? The proud granny wants to show off the baby.'

'Si, but first,' Almeida squeezed past Kara and hurried over to the Indian woman. Asking permission, which was regally granted, Almeida bent to look at the tiny form, and glancing up, Kara couldn't help smiling to see the two women, heads close, united in their awe and admiration of a new life which so nearly hadn't been.

Then, patting the woman's arm, and with a warm smile at the drowsy girl, Almeida bustled importantly out of the ward. A few moments later the shutters were unlocked and as they were pulled back, instead of afternoon sunlight, Kara was surprised to see that it was almost dark. Though she had been noting the time every fifteen minutes over the past two hours, she hadn't related it to the passage of day into evening.

The Indian woman went to the window and held up the baby. There was no sound but the steady rhythm of the generator motor. The woman brought the baby back to her daughter and helped her put it to her breast, murmuring softly words that Kara, still busy, could not hear.

As Almeida came back in, so without a word the Indian woman slipped out. 'Señora, all the people, they gone away now. They see the baby and they go quietly to village,' she shrugged.

Was that what they had been waiting for? Not for themselves, but to make sure mother and baby were all right? But what if they hadn't been? What if one or the other had died, as had seemed inevitable only hours ago?

Snap out of it, Kara scolded herself. Nothing did go wrong, and both have survived. Then why wasn't she feeling more elated? Why wasn't she bursting with pride, with adrenalin-charged energy?

'Make up the other bed in the ward will you, Almeida? And prepare a cot for the baby and curtain them off. They'll have to stay here at least a week. After all they've been through I'm taking no chances with either of them.'

Mother and baby were asleep, the boys settled for the night, and the theatre cleaned and prepared for the following day when Kara flopped onto the settee. She stretched her legs out towards the flames in the hearth and let her head fall back against the cool leather. Her eyes closed as exhaustion washed over her.

Almeida bustled in. 'You eat now, Señora?'

Kara shook her head. 'I'm not hungry.'

Almeida frowned and tutted. 'Come now, Señora. This very busy day for you, and you no sleep good last night, we none did. What will Señor Ross say?'

Kara's eyes snapped open, blazing with anger and torment as she swivelled round. 'I don't care a damn what Ross Hallam says. He's a liar, a hypocrite and he's trying to destroy this clinic. So don't try to blackmail me, Almeida! Just bring me some yoghurt and fruit, and if you want to keep your job, don't mention his name again.'

Shock, bewilderment and deep hurt chased each other across Almeida's plump face. Then with an ultra-polite, 'Si, Señora,' she sailed out, mortally offended, her chin so high she could barely see where she was going.

Kara opened her mouth to call her back, to explain, but the door closed with firm finality before she could utter a word. Hunching her body forward to try and ease the pain, Kara clasped her face in her hands. Hot tears slid through her fingers. Her shoulders heaved and shook, but not a sound escaped her as she tore apart inside.

In a little while the paroxysm subsided and Kara became dimly aware of murmuring in the kitchen. Vicente must be back. Had the Indians wrecked the lower plots too? Had Vicente managed to save any of the plants?

Kara scrubbed her face with her hanky and blew her nose. Almeida would bring in her supper in a moment. She smoothed back her hair, tucking the loose tendrils behind her ears. Her cheeks were burning and her eyes felt swollen and full of sand. She was so tired. If only she could just lie down, go to sleep and never wake up again, it would solve all her problems. A nice, tidy, simple, cowardly cop-out. Yes, you're tired, she told herself, and you're hurt. But what did you expect, falling in love with a total stranger? There are four patients in that ward, all totally dependent on you. Now get something to eat, get some rest, and get on with your job.

She prized herself, stiff and aching, off the settee and, feeling slightly light-headed, opened the door into the kitchen. 'Almeida, I'm sorry. I should not have said—' She stopped, her mouth falling open.

Ross stood in his socks in front of the fire, beside which his boots steamed gently. His hair was plastered to his scalp and he held a towel. His oilskin gleamed in the lamp and firelight where it hung, dripping, on the back door, and his trousers were dark with water from thigh to ankle.

'You're wet.' Kara said the first thing that came into her head, finding it hard to believe her own eyes. What was he doing here? How had he got back so soon?

'I got caught in the storm,' he replied evenly, but his features were set in lines of cold fury.

Kara had not heard the rain, for she had been involved in a storm of her own, but it must have been violent to have soaked him like that. She glanced at the housekeeper who immediately devoted herself to slicing bread, giving the task so much attention that Kara knew at once that she had repeated to Ross the words that had spilled out in her devastating grief.

Kara turned away. She needed time to think. She hadn't expected him back for another day at least. She wasn't prepared.

'Where do you think you're going?' The words were ground out like sand between two rock faces, and as Kara looked up her apprehension turned to real fear. She spun round and dived through the door, hoping to reach her bedroom, but he was too quick for her.

She was only half-way across the sitting room when his hand clamped on her upper arm. 'Oh no, you don't!' He yanked her to a halt and pulled her towards him. 'Now what the hell has been going on here?'

'Almeida—' Kara called, but as the housekeeper appeared in the doorway, her face alive with curiosity, Ross said over his shoulder,

'I'll handle this, Almeida. You just close the door and get on with whatever you're doing.'

'Almeida, you work for me,' Kara protested hotly.

Almeida tilted her chin. 'You said you fire me,' she retorted and closed the door.

'A liar and a hypocrite, am I? Out to destroy the clinic? Just what have I missed?' Ross grated.

'Don't tell me you don't know,' Kara hissed at him.

'Almeida started babbling something about the Indians getting drunk and stoning the clinic.'

'They also destroyed the crops. But of course, you only know what Almeida's told you,' Kara said with heavy sarcasm.

'That's right,' Ross's voice was deadly quiet. 'I only know what she's told me, because I wasn't here.'

'No, you made sure of that, didn't you?' Kara tried to wrench her arm free, but his hand tightened like a vice.

'What in God's name are you talking about?'

'Don't take me for a fool! Isn't that what you once said to me?' Kara hurled the words at him. 'Now I'm telling *you.* Was she worth it? Did you get your reward? Or would you have preferred thirty pieces of silver? That's the usual rate for betrayal, I believe.'

Ross stared at her, his mouth a hard line. The seconds ticked by and Kara felt dread mounting in her. He looked as though he could kill her.

She stopped struggling and stood still, holding her ground, but with the growing sensation that she was on quicksand.

'You think *I* was behind what happened here?' There was an odd, discordant note in Ross's voice, but Kara was too wretched to recognise it for what it was.

'What else can I think?' she whispered. 'Beatriz made it obvious at the dinner party she was determined to get you on their side.'

'And I thought I'd made my feelings on the matter quite clear,' Ross cut in icily.

'Oh yes, you had me convinced,' Kara cried, 'but then Beatriz turns up here just as you are leaving. Quite a coincidence, don't you think? And I reach the door just in time to hear you say you don't want me to see her. Then without a word of explanation, not even a good-bye, you ride off together. Where does that leave me? What am I supposed to think?'

Ross released her arm, as though to touch her was distasteful. 'And that's your evidence against me? All that I've—*no*,' he corrected himself, 'all that *we've* done here together since I arrived, wasn't sufficient proof of my interest in the clinic?'

Kara was tormented. She longed so desperately to believe him, but how could she?'

'It proved you were interested all right. But on whose behalf? Mine, the UN's or the family's?'

Ross stared at her bleakly, then lifted one end of the

towel he had slung around his neck and rubbed it over his dripping hair.

'I can't force you to believe anything I say. I will tell you what I learned and you must make up your own mind,' he said quietly. 'We didn't get the drugs because Beatriz cancelled the order.'

'Beatriz? She admitted it?' Kara was shaken.

Ross nodded. 'She had guessed that if they didn't arrive then sooner or later I would have to go down to find out why.'

'But she couldn't have been sure you would go. What if it had been me?'

'Had it been you, an "accident" would have been arranged—but she was counting on my sense of chivalry,' Ross's lip curled sardonically, 'which would have left you alone here, except for Almeida and Vicente. Only she couldn't wait. She was so eaten up with bitterness and jealousy she decided to get at you through the Indians.'

Kara swallowed. 'The whisky?'

Ross nodded once more. 'She knew the brujo would be resentful of your growing influence. It was a simple matter for her to stir him up more, then for the vaqueros to leave whisky at a prearranged spot.'

'But why did she come to the clinic, surely she would know I'd suspect her?'

Ross's smile was devoid of humour. 'That was the clever bit. She knew her appearance would make you suspicious, not only of her, but of me as well.' Kara flushed deeply as she realised how perfectly she had played into Beatriz's hands. Ross went on, 'The fact that I was leaving as she arrived was a real bonus for her. Not only did it look as though we'd planned it, it also ensured I'd be out of the way and unable to help when the trouble started.'

A yawning chasm opened beneath Kara's feet as all her accusations and certainties dissolved like morning mist. 'But—but you said you didn't want me to see her, I heard you.'

'You've got that the wrong way around,' he said coldly. 'What I actually said was I didn't want her to see you. I wanted to spare you any more unhappiness and aggravation. You are no match for the Beatriz's of this world, you're not spiteful or cynical enough—' his mouth twisted in self-mockery, '—or so I thought.'

Kara flinched as the shaft hit home. 'But why didn't you explain? Anyway, what reason did she give for coming?'

'A personal plea from Dona Elena. It seems Don Garcia has had a stroke and is dying and Dona Elena wishes my advice on certain matters,' Ross said without expression. 'We'll never know if the message was genuine. Beatriz would have put the idea to Dona Elena in such a way that the poor woman, ill and worried, would think it her own. As for my lack of explanation,' he ticked the reasons off on his fingers, 'there was no time. It would have raised more questions than I could answer just then, and Beatriz would have known I suspected her. To find out exactly what she was up to I had no choice but to play it her way and hope you had enough faith to trust me until I got back.' He shrugged, pulling the towel from his neck. 'Obviously I overestimated the strength of our relationship.' The blood burned hot in Kara's cheeks, she was utterly confused. 'Anyway,' Ross went on briskly, 'there will be no more trouble from Beatriz.'

'How can you be so sure?' Kara was plainly doubtful.

'Several reasons. I've warned her that one more incident, just the vaguest suspicion, and I'll have her blacklisted by every society hostess in the capital.'

'Can you do that?'

He nodded solemnly. 'She's not the only one with connections. I can do it. What is more, she knows I can, and for someone like Beatriz, to be a social outcast would be a fate worse than death.'

'And the other reasons?'

'Sit down,' he directed. 'I may as well give you the lot now, though this wasn't how I had—' He stopped, and rubbed the towel roughly over his face and hair once more before tossing it over the back of a chair.

'Shouldn't you change first?' Kara suggested tentatively. 'You look awfully wet.'

He glanced over his shoulder at her. 'How touching. One minute I'm every kind of bastard, the next you're concerned for my comfort.'

She flushed vividly at his biting cynicism.

'I'll survive a few minutes longer.'

Kara sat in the corner of the big settee, her back against the arm, hugging her bent knees, making of them a kind of barrier. She didn't know what to think or believe any more. She was aware that she had done Ross a grave and terrible injustice, yet at the same time her fear and mistrust had not been wholly unjustified. There was so much she simply did not know.

Ross lowered himself onto the other end and rested one arm along the back, crossing his legs. 'While I was in Quito, as well as sorting out the drugs, which I've brought back with me, I had a meeting with Francisco and Medina and we've reached an agreement. I've had a notary draw up a document which permits a compromise over the will. The family undertake to drop all legal action to prove the will invalid, they will also relinquish all claim to the clinic and the land on which it stands if you will agree to waive all claim to the residue of the estate.'

'But if I do that, how—'

'Let me finish,' Ross cut in crisply. 'I have completed my assessment of the clinic and though everything connected with it has been fraught with problems,' he gave her a look which curled her toes, 'it does fulfil certain necessary criteria, and the UN will take it over.'

It was several seconds before Kara fully understood what he had said. It was all over. The decision was made. The clinic was safe!

'Thank you,' she said quietly, and slid her feet to the floor, half-turning away, clasping her hands tightly in her lap. Her lips were dry and she had to moisten them with the tip of her tongue before she could go on. 'I assume the UN will want to appoint someone of their own choosing to take charge?'

He nodded. 'I have someone in mind, as a matter of fact. This chap's in his mid-thirties, well-qualified, has worked extensively in South America as well as other parts of the world. Having done a lot of travelling he's looking for a chance to settle somewhere and put down a few roots.' Kara looked at him. 'Large hospitals and specialisation have never appealed to him, he's much more interested in the challenge and variety of back-woods medicine.'

Was she imagining it, or did he really mean . . . 'You?' she whispered.

He nodded, and gave a strangely diffident shrug, the ghost of a smile deepening the lines at the corner of his mouth.

She didn't know what to say, how to react. If he had told her before he went, her joy would have been unbounded. But of course he couldn't have told her then because the meetings had not taken place. But so much had happened in that brief absence, nothing was the same any more. Only an hour ago she had believed him to be responsible for the drunken orgy of destruction by the Indians. She had believed it against her will, still loving him, no longer knowing who to trust.

Now, not only had he told her that Beatriz was behind all that and had been dealt with, but he had also solved the problems with the family, the will, and now wanted, on behalf of the UN, to take over running the clinic. It was all too much to absorb at once. She stood up, not looking at him. 'If you'll excuse me—'

In one lithe movement he was on his feet, towering over her, his hands gentle on her shoulders, spinning her round to face him. 'Nothing to say?' His tone was mildly mocking, but his dark eyes held a reserve, a totally uncharacteristic uncertainty that Kara, in her distraction did not notice.

'What do you want me to say?' she blurted. 'Of course I'm glad the decision's been made. I've always believed the clinic was vital to the community, so I'm glad you've decided to—'

Ross shook his head impatiently, 'I don't want your gratitude.' His hands tightened on her shoulders, 'I want,' he hesitated, 'I want you to marry me,' he said roughly.

Her head snapped up. She felt the blood drain from her face, and the floor tilted. 'What?' she murmured faintly. She had misheard, he couldn't have said it.

'You heard me well enough,' he grated. 'I asked you to marry me.'

She stared at him for a long moment. She loved him. Nothing, not her doubts, mistaken beliefs nor the terrors of the previous night had altered that. She would always love him. But what of his feelings for her? He had never mentioned any, apart from calling her an 'impossible woman'. So, assuming he did not love her, why would he propose marriage? To keep her here? To protect her reputation and make it easier for her to stay on? To acquire a working partner? Was that all she was to him? All she would ever be? Hadn't she already travelled that road once?

'No,' she sobbed, her face a mask of anguish. She tore herself free. 'No.' And before Ross could move she had fled, stumbling to her bedroom.

'Kara!' Ross raced after her but the door closed in his face, the key turning in the lock.

'Kara,' he repeated softly, but there was no answer.

CHAPTER NINE

KARA LAY on her back in the darkness. She would begin packing in the morning. She could not possibly stay now. At least the clinic and its patients would be in good hands. The best.

Tears slid from Kara's eyes, ran down her temples and soaked into her hair. How ironic that despite the legal agreement and the UN's take-over, the family had won after all. She was leaving. It wasn't their tactics of terror or deprivation that were finally driving her away, it was a proposal of marriage from the man she loved. How Beatriz would laugh.

There was a knock at the door. Kara didn't answer. Then Almeida's voice called, 'Señora? I have hot water for you.'

Dashing the tears away, Kara swung her legs off the bed and went wearily to the door.

'The Señor, he gone to see brujo,' Almeida couldn't wait to confide as she poured out the pitcherful of water. 'He say the brujo give drink to the men, make them drunk to give you trouble. The Señor he say he sort him out.' She frowned as she grappled with the unfamiliar phrase. 'What is this "sort him out"? And why you lie in the dark? I fetch lamp.'

'I think he's going to tell the brujo that things are going to be very different from now on, and that he will be running the clinic in future. I was lying in the dark because my eyes are tired.'

'Is that why you cry?' Almeida asked shrewdly, bringing in a lamp and lighting Kara's with a taper. Then it dawned. 'Señor Ross is staying? Señor Ross run the clinic?' Delight spread over her face like a ray of sunlight. 'Señora, that is wonderful, you and he together—'

'No,' Kara cut her short, the vision conjured by Almeida's words was too beautiful and too full of pain to be borne. 'Not together. I shall be leaving.'

Almeida's mouth fell open in shock and dismay. 'Is not true,' she shook her head. 'Is not possible you leave. This your home! You work so hard—why? Why you leave?'

Kara put her hand over her eyes and leaned against the wall by the wash stand. 'He asked me to marry him, Almeida,' she croaked, her voice harsh with tears.

'Ah Señora, is wonderful, perfect.'

'No, it isn't,' Kara shook her head, 'Oh, you don't understand.'

'Is true, I no understand,' Almeida was sharp in her perplexity. 'He good man, strong in his body and his mind—'

'But I mean nothing to him. He doesn't love me—'

'What you saying?' Almeida snorted contemptuously. 'That man love you from first day he come here. Oh, he don't know it then, but I see, I know. I see what in his eyes, in his heart. I see him fight it.'

Kara raised her tear-stained face. 'What are you talking about?'

Almeida snorted again. 'I see him watch you when you don't know. I see war in him. He have women,' she shrugged, 'maybe many women, but he a man alone, no woman take his heart before. But you have it, and now you throw it down, like food for the pigs.'

'That's ridiculous,' Kara tried to scoff, 'you're imagining all this.' But a tiny, desperate glimmer of hope stirred in the blackness that filled her soul.

'Señora,' Almeida placed a hand on her vast bosom, with great solemnity, 'I swear by Our Lady and all the Blessed Saints, I tell truth. Señor Ross, he love you.'

'Then why didn't he tell me? If only he had said—'

'Did *you* say? Did you tell him what in *your* heart?'

Almeida demanded, thrusting her face forward, the pitcher clasped in one hand, while the other rested on her bulky hip.

Kara shook her head and shrugged helplessly. 'I couldn't—I—'

Almeida sighed crossly. 'Sometimes I think you no deserve man like him.'

'You don't understand,' Kara cried miserably.

Almeida reached up to cup Kara's pale face in one work-roughened hand. 'I see your fear,' she said softly. 'I see you unhappy with Señor Luis. He no give you the love a woman needs. I see you alone since he die, you work so hard to forget the sadness. Señor Ross come and you afraid he bring more sadness. Is wrong, *querida*.'

The endearment touched Kara deeply. Almeida was not simply a servant, she was a dear and trusted friend, a rock of common sense and loyal affection.

'You must not run from life. You have had much grief, but you are strong. To find happiness you must risk sorrow. But you and Señor Ross—is good.' Almeida busily transferred the pitcher from one hand to the other. 'Now you wash, then come and eat.'

'Yes, Almeida,' Kara agreed meekly.

She was sitting at the kitchen table, facing the fire, toying with the spoon in her empty dish. She yearned for Ross to return. Surely he wouldn't be much longer. There was so much to talk about, so much she had to explain.

The warm glow that suffused her body turned chill as she realised how close she had come to disaster. Blinded by her fear she might have slipped away, never knowing that he—she still couldn't bring herself to say it. She needed to hear it from his own lips, longed for the confirming pressure of his mouth on hers, his arms holding her close . . .

The door crashed open and Kara spun round, joy blazing in her eyes, but it was Vicente who stumbled in.

'*Upa anca*,' he panted, his face grey and beaded with the sweat of fear.

Translated literally the words meant the silent swoop of an eagle onto its prey, but throughout the Andes they were used to describe a particularly horrific form of landslide. Without warning and without a sound, the earth would suddenly let go, enveloping everything in its path.

The room spun. Kara was hurled back twelve months, to a night just like this, dark and misty after heavy rain. And when she had got there it had been too late, Luis was dead, suffocated beneath the tons of earth, mud and stone that blocked the path, scarring the hillside like a great jagged wound.

Not again. It could not happen again! God could not be so cruel . . .

Feeling as though she were trapped in a ghastly nightmare where everything was happening in slow motion, Kara got up, kicking back her chair. It fell over and bounced on the floor. 'Ross!' Her throat was so tight with dread, the sound emerged as a groan.

Heedless of her nightclothes, her hair flying loose about her shoulders, Kara flung herself out of the door and raced down the path with Vicente close behind her. Her sheepskin slippers were soaked in seconds and the stones on the path bruised her feet and threatened to turn her ankles. She ran faster than she had ever run in her life.

She flew through the village and past the houses, which all seemed to be empty. Further on she could see torches, the flames bobbing in the mist like fire-flies. She heard the murmur of voices and within moments had reached the knot of people and was fighting her way through.

Several men were already digging away the wet, sticky earth with their hands. Others joined them moments later with crude picks and shovels. The women held the torches, moving this way and that in response to the calls of the men as they dug. The air was moist and cold and held a whiff of corruption. The tang of cheap, stale whisky mingled with the rank stench of wet earth.

Reaching the front, Kara froze. 'Ross!' she screamed, wildly searching for some sign of his tall figure. There was no reply. The digging stopped and men straightened up. Someone scrambled over the lower edge of the fall.

'Ross?' her voice cracked, and she leapt forward, shaking off Vicente's restraining grip.

'Kara?' The mud-caked figure stood upright and Kara flung herself into his arms, laughing and crying, tears glistening like diamonds on her ashen cheeks as she clung to him, trembling uncontrollably.

'I thought—I thought,' she choked, unable to voice the dread that had haunted her in those endless seconds since Vicente had entered the kitchen.

Ross's arms closed around her, holding her so tightly he lifted her off the ground. She raised her face and his rough beard scraped her cheek.

'Kara,' he grated.

'Oh Ross, I love you,' she sobbed, 'if anything had happened to you I couldn't have borne it.'

'Hush, hush, it's all right.' His body was as taut as a steel hawser as he crushed her to him.

After a moment, suddenly aware of their blank-faced audience, Kara pulled free, brushing her tears away with a shaky hand. 'Oh God, a fine doctor I am,' she murmured in self-disgust, 'I haven't brought a thing with me! Is anyone hurt?'

'There was only one casualty,' Ross said quietly, 'the brujo, and he's dead.' Behind him several men appeared over the fall, carrying a body wrapped in a blanket.

'What happened?' Kara's teeth chattered as reaction set in and the damp night air cut through her thin garments.

'He'd been drinking,' Ross said grimly, 'and when I

told him that I was taking over the clinic, that if he put one foot out of line I'd have him jailed, and that free booze in exchange for intimidation was out as from now, he went for me. We had a bit of a struggle and I slipped and fell. He smashed the end off the bottle he was holding, but as he was about to come in for the kill, he suddenly stopped and staggered backwards. Then he looked up. He opened his mouth, but before he could make a sound, the hillside collapsed on him.'

Kara shuddered. Whatever the brujo had done, it was a terrible way to die.

'Come on,' Ross said brusquely, 'there's nothing more we can do here tonight.' He put his arm around her shoulder, squeezing it gently every few moments, as though assuring himself she was real.

Ross had bathed in the wash-house and now wore a clean pair of navy cords and a pale blue wool shirt. His tanned skin glowed from the scrubbing and Kara could smell the fresh tang of his soap.

She had needed to change her wet and mud-stained nightclothes, but in an unaccountable fit of shyness, instead of putting on a fresh nightdress and her spare bathrobe, she had dug into the chest to find an ankle-length caftan of dusty-rose velour, scented faintly with gardenia. Emerging from her room, more than a little nervous, she had been startled to find Ross waiting for her, his arms full of boxes.

'Come and help me unpack this lot and bring me up to date on the medical front,' he said quietly. 'Almeida tells me we have two new in-patients.'

Kara was filled with gratitude. He seemed to know without being told that she needed a little while to adjust, to be with him and talk about other things before they plunged into what was really on their minds.

Kara examined the labels on the drug boxes and bottles and entered them in the stock list as Ross unpacked them, then she put them away in the cupboard.

She related the day's happenings and showed him the notes. As she took the folder back, he caught her left wrist and lifted her hand, looking at the pale mark on her finger.

'Why?' he demanded.

She met his gaze openly. 'Why did I take it off? Because the past is gone and I cannot go on living still chained to something I know now never existed.'

'Why did you turn me down?'

Kara looked at the floor for an instant, her hair falling forward in a golden curtain. 'Because I didn't know what your feelings were. You had never said.' She forced herself to meet his eyes, eyes that held a tenderness she had never seen before, and she knew she could tell him everything. 'I was so afraid you had asked me for the wrong reasons.'

He looked puzzled. 'The wrong reasons?'

Kara nodded, grimacing slightly. 'You were always so concerned for my reputation. I thought it might be because you wanted a working partner, and I know both the job and the people. But I couldn't have done it, not again, not after Luis—especially as I—'

Ross pulled her roughly towards him. 'You little fool. I asked you to marry me because I love you, because I can't envisage life without you and because being here, living and working together the way we are, is not enough, would never be enough.' He shrugged, shaking his head. 'God knows, I wasn't prepared for this. I refused to admit it was happening at first.'

Kara, recalling Almeida's words, was filled with wonder. Her heart swelled with love as she saw beneath Ross's facade of cool, distant arrogance to the heart of the man, as bewildered as she by what had happened to them both, as uncertain, longing to speak but fearing rejection.

'I never knew,' Kara whispered, 'I never realised.' She lifted her face and rubbed his cheek softly. Ross turned his head and sought her lips in a tender, cherishing kiss that sent Kara's heart soaring.

Ross gently tugged her hair, pulling her head back. 'So you will marry me?' he demanded.

'You wouldn't rather we just lived together?' Kara teased, her eyes dancing.

'No,' he was adamant. 'I've never felt like this before. Dammit, I've never proposed before and now I've actually got around to it, it's got to be right. Total commitment, vows, a certificate to prove it, the whole bit, all or nothing.

Kara's smile was radiant. 'I'll take it.'

There was a soft tap on the door. Kara wriggled free of Ross's embrace and went to open it.

'You want I do first shift watching mother and baby?' Almeida enquired innocently. Her black eyes darted from one to the other, noting Kara's rosy glow and Ross's broad grin.

Uncertain, Kara turned to Ross. But before she could speak he replied, 'You can manage temperature and pulse readings?'

Almeida drew herself up. 'Of course, Señor. I done this many times. You give the watch please.' She held out her hand. Ross unbuckled his watch and gave it her. 'Then the patients are in your capable hands.' He smiled to soften the proviso, 'But any problems at all—'

'Si, Señor, I call you,' Almeida promised.

'Come on,' Ross slipped his arm around Kara's waist, 'let's call it a day.' He gave her a squeeze, 'I'm hungry.'

'You want I cook you something, Señor?' Almeida offered.

To Kara's surprise Ross leaned down and whispered in Almeida's ear. She pursed her lips, gave him a sideways look and turned to waddle out into the ward, trying not to grin.

Ross and Kara followed, leaning over to check the boys and peeping in at the mother and baby, both sleeping peacefully. Almeida was settled on a chair beneath the lamp, Ross's watch strapped on her wrist, and already she had some sewing in her plump hands as they passed her.

Kara turned towards the kitchen but Ross pulled her back, running his hands from her shoulders down her back and over the curve of her hips, moulding her against him. Her arms twined round his neck and her body responded instantly, joyfully, to the powerful, tightly controlled pressure. She quivered as warmth flooded her, a delicious sensuality that tingled from her scalp to her toes. 'But—but your meal?' Kara smiled, slightly breathless.

His dark eyes gleamed, growing larger and deeper until she felt she would drown in them. He swept her up in his arms. 'Who mentioned food?' he growled huskily. 'I said I was hungry.'

The bedroom door closed softly on their mingled laughter.